Shark Attack!

Danny, Joe, and Irene gazed out the window of the deep-diving ship at a monstrous blue-green shape.

"A shark," whispered Danny. "It's almost as big as the ship."

"Danny! Do something!" cried Irene suddenly. "It's going to attack that fish."

Danny rushed to the stern and thrust his arms into the metal sleeves that controlled the jointed arms and claws outside the ship.

As the shark approached, Danny raised one of the arms. He hit the shark hard, but the monster turned and swam straight for the ship. . . .

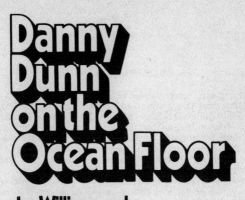

Danny Dunn on the Ocean Floor

Jay Williams and Raymond Abrashkin

Illustrated by Brinton Turkle

AN ARCHWAY PAPERBACK
POCKET BOOKS • NEW YORK

Acknowledgments

The authors are deeply grateful to Dr. Bruce C. Heezen of the Lamont Geological Observatory for his assistance; to W. Clois Ensor for advice about complicated musical matters; to the Mexican Government Tourist Bureau for much information about Mexico; to Moses Asch for allowing us to study the sounds of fish on recordings of the Science Series of Folkways Records and Service Corporation; and to Mary Cock and Reginald Weedon for their courtesy in providing working space.

We also wish to acknowledge our profound indebtedness to the writings of the pioneers of deep-sea exploration: Dr. William Beebe, Professor Auguste Piccard, Captain Jacques-Yves Cousteau, and Lieutenant Commander George Huout.

POCKET BOOKS, a Simon & Schuster division of
GULF & WESTERN CORPORATION
1230 Avenue of the Americas, New York, N.Y. 10020

Copyright © 1960 by Jay Williams and Raymond Abrashkin

Published by arrangement with McGraw-Hill, Inc.
Library of Congress Catalog Card Number: 60-12786

ISBN: 0-671-29967-0

First Pocket Books printing June, 1979

10 9 8 7 6 5 4 3 2

Trademarks registered in the United States and other countries.

Printed in the U.S.A.

This book is for
Mike Burnham, Jr.
and also for
Katie Meadow

"Nothing is impossible. Some things
are just harder to believe than others."

—Professor Euclid Bullfinch

Contents

1
The Sounds of Fish

Professor Euclid Bullfinch hummed cheerily to himself as he set a large crucible—a pot made to withstand high heat—in the furnace that filled one corner of his laboratory.

He checked the temperature setting and shut the furnace. Then he seated himself at one of the stone-topped laboratory benches. He opened his notebook and for a moment chewed the end of his fountain pen as he looked thoughtfully out the open window. The sweet scent of honeysuckle came from his garden, along with the murmur of bees, and the Professor drew a deep contented breath.

Then he wrote, "Mixture placed in oven,

1

10:21, 300°. Why has no one tried this approach to this type of plastic before? Perhaps the results will not justify—''

The laboratory door flew open. A red-headed boy and a pretty girl with a dark pony-tail flying behind her burst into the room. ''Professor!'' the boy shouted. ''We need your help!''

Professor Bullfinch looked up over the rims of his glasses. Then, in a mild tone, he said, ''Shut the door, please, Danny.'' When, a little sheepishly, the boy had done so, the Professor put down his pen and went on, ''I perceive from the calm way in which you stopped to obey me that there's no emergency. No one has drowned, or burned up, or been swallowed in an earthquake, I take it?''

''Oh, no, nothing like that,'' said Danny Dunn. He rubbed his snub nose and added, ''Gee, Professor, I see what you mean. I guess we shouldn't have come busting in like that. I'm sorry. I just didn't stop to think.''

The girl, whose name was Irene Miller, said, ''Oh, dear, I hope we haven't interrupted any important work. We'd better come back another time, Dan.''

''No, no,'' the Professor protested with a smile. ''I merely wished to point out that it's too warm a day for unnecessary bustling about. Sit down, both of you. I have been experimenting with a new type of plastic."

"Is it for Dr. Grimes's project?" Danny asked.

"Yes. He should be here soon, and I hope to have the answer to one of his problems."

The two young people sat down, and Danny carefully set a small case on one of the benches. It contained a battery-operated tape recorder which he had assembled from a kit with Irene's help.

Danny was greatly interested in science, and knew much more about its principles than most boys of his age. His father had died when he was very young, and his mother had taken a post as housekeeper for Professor Bullfinch. Danny had grown up under the wing of the famous scientist, who had taught him a great deal, and the Professor felt as much affection for Danny as if the boy were his own son. Irene lived next door. Her father was an astronomer who taught at Midston, the local university, and she, too, had the ambition of becoming a scientist when she grew up.

She said, now, "If you're sure we're not interrupting, Professor. . . . Go ahead, Dan. Tell the Professor about your theory."

A series of grunts came from the machine.

"I'll do more than that," Danny grinned. "I'll play it for you."

The scientist sat back and lit his pipe. "Play it?" he asked. "Is it a theory about music?"

Danny shook his head. He pulled the tape recorder out of its case. It had its own tiny amplifier, which he turned on, and then he threw the battery switch. At once, from the miniature machine, came a series of grunts that sounded like a cross between a pig and the plunking of a bass fiddle.

The Professor raised his eyebrows. "It certainly *isn't* music," he said. "But what is it?"

"A fish," said Danny.

"It's a toadfish," Irene added. "Isn't it lovely?"

"I . . . don't . . . think . . . so," said the Professor slowly. "Interesting? Yes. Odd? Yes. Lovely? No."

Irene giggled. "Well, I was just thinking of that little fish floating in the sea and grunting happily to himself. That's kind of lovely, isn't it?"

"I see what you mean." The Professor nodded.

"We've got a whole lot of them," Danny said.

"What on earth do you plan to do with a

whole lot of toadfish?'' asked the Professor. "And where do you keep them?"

"No, not toadfish," said Danny. "A lot of fish sounds. On tape."

"Really? You don't look wet."

"We haven't been in the water. We got them from your friend, Dr. Brenton, at the University," Danny said. "He's been doing experiments in animal behavior. Nobody knew until recently that fish made any sounds, but the Naval Research Laboratory recorded some, and so did Dr. Brenton. He let me tape them from his recordings."

"Ah, yes, I seem to have heard of those experiments," said the Professor. "Very interesting. You said you wanted my help. Do you want me to get you some live fish?"

"Nothing like that, Professor." Danny leaned forward earnestly. "Here's my theory. I've been listening to the different sounds, and I think there's a definite pattern to them. If we could figure it out, we might be able to understand the language of fish!"

The Professor drew in a mouthful of smoke and let it trickle slowly between his lips. "My dear boy," he said at last, "mere patterns of sound don't make a language. We must be sure they go along with specific actions or meanings. For instance, all the songs of birds may or may not be language. But crows do communicate with each other by means of certain cries. They warn each other; they tell when an owl is present—these cries might perhaps be called a language of a sort.''

Danny said, ''I see. Well, listen to this.''

Again he turned on his recorder. This time there came a series of short barks.

''That's a sea catfish,'' he explained.

''Sounds as though he's imitating a sea dogfish,'' the Professor remarked.

''He's being held in someone's hand,'' said Danny. ''So that might be a fear sound or a threatening sound.''

''The sounds seem to fall into groups,'' Irene put in. ''Some are clicks; some are grunts; some are soft whistles or beeps—''

''She can hear tones I can't make out at all,'' Danny said admiringly. ''She has a better ear than I have.''

''Let us apply the scientific method,'' said the Professor, putting his fingertips together. ''To begin with, we ought to classify the sounds. Suppose you play them, Dan. And Irene, you repeat them and tell me what they are. Then we can sort them out.''

He took a sheet of paper and drew several

columns on it. At the tops of the columns he wrote CLICKS, BEEPS, CHIRPS, WHISTLES, GRUNTS.

"That's enough to start with," he said. "Go on, Danny—begin."

A short time later, Danny's mother, Mrs. Dunn, entered the lab with a tray of oatmeal cookies and lemonade. "I thought you might—" she began, and stopped short, with her mouth still open.

Irene, sitting on a laboratory bench, was going, *"Quirp? Pleeoop! Quirp!"*

Professor Bullfinch, rubbing his chin, said, *"Quirp?"*

Danny, dancing about excitedly, cried, "No, no. More like this: *Wheerp! Wheerp!"*

"Professor," said Mrs. Dunn.

He nodded absently and said, "Perhaps, *queerp?"*

"Danny!" Mrs. Dunn said.

"Yes, Mom?" said Danny. *"Queerp, queerp!"*

"Dear me," said Mrs. Dunn. "If you're all feverish, you'd better not eat anything. I'll just take these cookies back to the kitchen."

Danny ran to her and threw his arms around her. "No!" he shouted. "You couldn't be so cruel. I'm sorry. We were working on fish sounds."

8

"Ah, so that's what it was," said Mrs. Dunn, her blue eyes twinkling. "Fish sounds? Well, here's one for you: *Crkl-crkl-crkl!*"

"I give up," said Danny. "What is it, Mom?"

"Frying fish," laughed his mother.

"Splendid," said the Professor. "That's one your friend Joe Pearson would like, Dan. Isn't he an expert on food?"

"Speaking of food," said Mrs. Dunn, "don't I smell something burning? I don't think I have anything in the oven. . . ."

The Professor sprang to his feet, clapping a hand to his rosy, bald head. "Great heavens!" he cried. "My plastic! I forgot all about it!"

2
Cooking Chemicals

They could all smell it now—a strong, smoky, faintly sweetish odor. Professor Bullfinch sprang to the furnace and pulled open the door.

"Ah, me," he sighed. "This goose is certainly cooked."

As the two young people drew closer, he fished the crucible out with a long iron hook. The pot had turned dark brown, and the stuff in it was smoking.

"Is it ruined?" Danny asked.

"I'm afraid so. However, it won't be too hard to duplicate the mixture."

The Professor opened the window to let the fumes escape. At that moment the wall telephone rang. Mrs. Dunn answered it and, after speaking for a moment, hung up and said, "That was Dr. Grimes, Professor."

"Dr. Grimes? Where is he?"

"At the airport." Mrs. Dunn pulled the corners of her mouth down and, in a good imitation of Dr. Grimes's gruff tones, said, "Tell Bullfinch to come and fetch me. I don't trust the careless speeding of taxicabs."

They all laughed. "That sounds like Grimes," said the Professor. "He's planning to explore the bottom of the sea, but he's afraid of a taxi. I'll go at once. Dan, you and Irene may eat my share of the cookies."

He took his jacket from a peg behind the door. As he was putting it on, Danny said, "Professor, may Irene and I stay here in the lab and work on our list of fish noises?"

Professor Bullfinch stopped with one arm in a sleeve. "Danny," he said gently.

The boy blushed. "I know just what you're going to say," he protested. "You don't want me to do any experimenting while you're gone."

"We-e-ell," said the Professor, "the last time I left you alone in the lab you tried to launch a CO_2 rocket through the window without opening the window. It isn't that I don't trust you, my boy. It's just that you do have a habit of acting, sometimes, without thinking."

"I won't this time, Professor," said Danny.

"And I'll see that he does exactly what you tell him," Irene promised.

"Very well. As a matter of fact, there is something you can do for me," said Professor Bullfinch. "When the crucible is cool, you can throw the mixture out. Don't bother to clean the crucible; just leave it on the bench."

He bustled off, and Mrs. Dunn went back to her housework. Danny and Irene sat down once more with the tape recorder, the cookies, and the lemonade, listening to the strange sounds and trying to list them under the proper columns.

Every now and then Danny checked the crucible, and after fifteen minutes or so he decided that it was cool enough to handle. He was able to pick it up easily, and he carried it to the trash can. He tilted it and then he said, "Hey, Irene! This thing's empty."

She hurried to his side. "How can it be empty? I don't think plastic would evaporate."

"Look at it. It doesn't look as if there's anything in the pot." As he said this, he put his hand in it. He looked up at her with a puzzled air. "There *is* something," he said. "I can feel it, but it's transparent."

Irene touched the surface of the stuff. It had

13

a curious, velvety texture, not smooth like glass, so that it did not reflect the light well. This made it hard to see.

Danny tried tapping the bottom of the crucible to get the plastic out. Then he took a hammer and hit the clear material as hard as he could. The hammer bounced up as if it had struck stone.

"Perhaps you'd better leave it alone," Irene suggested. "You might break the crucible."

Danny pursed up his lips. "Let's just try the electric drill," he said. "That ought to do it."

He got out a power drill and fitted a high-speed bit into it. He started the motor and pressed the bit against the mysterious substance. The point of the bit skittered off and chipped a small piece out of the edge of the crucible.

"There," said Irene. "Now you'd better leave it alone."

Danny was examining the plastic. "This stuff isn't even scratched," he said. He picked up the crucible and carried it back to the furnace.

"What are you going to do?" Irene asked.

"Only one thing to do. I'll heat it up again."

"Danny!" said Irene warningly. "You've forgotten your promise."

Danny turned a pair of wide, perfectly

innocent blue eyes on her. "I have *not*," he answered. "This isn't experimenting. Professor Bullfinch told me to throw the stuff away, didn't he? And I can't throw it away when it's solid, can I? I'll have to heat it up to make it liquid so that it'll throw."

Irene thought about that for a moment and then said, "I guess you're right."

Danny put the crucible back in the furnace, and they both watched until curls of white steam began to rise from the plastic. Danny took a steel poker and touched the material. It rippled thickly, like molasses.

The crucible had two handles, and he got a pair of metal hooks and hooked them into the handles. He took one and Irene took the other, and they carefully lifted the melting pot out of the furnace.

"Now it's too hot to pour into the trash bin," Danny said. "Let's take it over to the window sill and let it cool for a minute or two."

Just as they were lifting it to the sill, there came a loud whistle. A thin dark boy with a mournful expression on his face had come into the garden. Under one arm he carried a football.

"Hi, Dan," he called. "Hello, Irene. Come on out."

"Can't, Joe," Danny replied, resting his elbows on the sill. "We're busy."

Joe Pearson, who was Danny's closest friend, eyed the crucible. "What's that thing?" he said. "A cooking pot? Or a chemical pot?"

"Both," Danny grinned. "We're cooking some chemicals."

Joe paused, and a wary look came over his face. "Oh—oh," he said. "Another experiment, eh? When is this one going to explode?"

"It isn't," said Danny. "This is Professor Bullfinch's experiment. I have to throw it away."

"Won't he mind?"

"Oh, Joe, don't be a glop," said Irene. "He *wants* us to throw it away."

"Why? Doesn't he like it any more?"

"It was an experiment that didn't work out."

"I see," Joe sighed. "There are lots of things about this I will never understand. Just tell me one thing. What's a glop?"

Irene laughed. "It's what you are when you talk foolishly."

"I get it. Looks to me as if we're all glops together. Well, when are you going to be finished with the throwing away? Because I just got this neat football from George Cahill in a trade. I swapped him my boxing gloves for it.''

They could see, now, that one of Joe's eyes was swollen and discolored.

"July is a little early for football, isn't it?" Danny asked.

"Oh, I'm doing my Christmas shopping early," said Joe airily. "Anyway, I didn't want the boxing gloves any more. Come on out, and we'll have a game.''

"Looks like a pretty good ball," Danny commented.

"In perfect condition," Joe tossed it up and caught it a few times. The sight was too tempting for Danny.

"Pitch it here," he said. "Let's see it.''

Joe drew back his arm.

"Danny," said Irene. "I really think that's—''

Joe threw the ball. Danny reached out for it. It hit his fingers and bounded sideways. With a soggy kind of splash, it fell directly into the crucible.

"—not a very good idea," Irene finished with a sigh.

3

"The Answer to All Your Problems!"

Professor Bullfinch led his friend, Dr. A. J. Grimes, into the front hall. They made an amusing pair—the Professor short, plump, and rosy, and Dr. Grimes tall and craggy, with a lean face that looked as if he were perpetually tasting something sour. He put his suitcase down and looked about the hall. In a harsh voice, he said, "Good to be here, Bullfinch."

The Professor smiled. He could tell—although no one else would have guessed—that Dr. Grimes was laughing heartily, for there were two tiny wrinkles at the corners of his mouth.

"Good to have you here, old man," said the

Professor. "Let's go into the lab before we get you settled. There's something I must check on."

Dr. Grimes rubbed his hands together. "One week of rest," he said, "and then to work. My deep-diving ship, Bullfinch, is going to be the most perfect undersea laboratory ever seen. All I have to do is work out a few—hrmph!—minor details."

"Yes, so you wrote me," said the Professor. "Minor problems! The type of metal to use to resist pressure, the question of space inside the vehicle, the problem of observation—"

"All very minor," Dr. Grimes interrupted. "Nothing to them. Within the year I'll be diving into the Pacific Ocean."

"I certainly hope you'll have the ship ready by the time you dive," murmured the Professor. "As I remember it, you're not a very good swimmer. However, I may have the plastic for the observation window ready for you."

Dr. Grimes put a lean hand on the Professor's shoulder. "Now look here, Bullfinch," he said. "You keep talking as if I were going without you. I'm not. Drat it, man, we don't always agree but I—well, I just couldn't go on an expedition like this and leave you home. I'd have no one to argue with!"

The Professor peered up into his friend's

face with a grin. "You touch me, Grimes," he said. "But I'm not surprised—I have been expecting this. Yes, and I'll admit I've been thinking about it for some time. Why shouldn't I go? It might be a pleasant vacation."

"Vacation? Don't be absurd. We'll be working hard. We might find a moment or two for relaxation, but no more. Well, what do you say?"

The Professor stroked his chin pensively. Then he said abruptly, "I'll do it!"

"Excellent," said Grimes, and they shook hands.

"Now, what about Danny?" asked the Professor, leading the way down the hall toward the laboratory. "It would be a wonderful trip for the boy."

Dr. Grimes scowled. "You know my views on children, Bullfinch. They are always in the way. And Danny is reckless and headstrong."

"I'll admit he sometimes jumps into things," the Professor murmured. "But then, he's a boy, after all. He is essentially very serious, very calm, quiet and reliable—"

As he said this, he threw wide the door. There came a crash of glass, and something hurtled through the air toward the two scientists. Instinctively, Dr. Grimes held up his hands. The object landed right in them.

21

Danny, Irene, and Joe stood wide-eyed in surprise. Danny held a hammer, and there were bits of broken test tubes scattered about from a rack that had fallen to the floor. Dr. Grimes looked down at the thing he had caught.

"A football!" he sputtered. "Playing football in a laboratory! Is that what you call calm and quiet, or serious and reliable?"

"Gosh, I'm sorry, Dr. Grimes," said Danny. "It was an accident."

"Do you expect us to believe you were playing football by accident?" cried Grimes.

"We weren't playing," Danny said. "We were trying to break it. I had just hit it with the hammer, and it flew off to one side and knocked over the test tubes and just happened to shoot toward you as you opened the door."

Professor Bullfinch blinked in a dazed fashion. "Just a moment, Dan," he said. "For some reason, the more you explain, the more confused I become. You say you were trying to break the ball? But you weren't playing with it? Why do you want to break it?"

"Professor," said Danny earnestly, "I don't think that ball *can* be broken. I think we've invented an unbreakable football!"

Professor Bullfinch slowly took the football from Dr. Grimes's hands and stared at it. Now he could see that the football itself had been deflated, and that it was inside a very thin shell of plastic. This shell, however, was shaped like a football. The Professor pressed it with his fingers. It was as rigid as steel.

"Perhaps you'd better explain," he said.

"Really, Bullfinch," Dr. Grimes began. "Do we have the time—?"

"My dear Grimes," said the Professor. "You are here for a rest. There's plenty of time. Go on, Danny."

Quickly, the boy explained how he had heated the plastic and cooled it again on the window sill, and how he had asked Joe to throw up the football without thinking that it might land in the crucible.

"When we fished it out," he said, "it was covered with plastic. We cleaned up the mess and then tried to get the plastic off the ball. There's one place, near the lacing, where there isn't any plastic—look, you can see it. Joe had the idea of letting the air out of the ball. So we did, but we still couldn't get the ball out. We tried hammering the plastic, but, although it's only about as thick as an eggshell, we couldn't even scratch it. We jumped on it and pounded it with a chair and I was just hammering it again when you walked in."

23

The Professor adjusted his glasses. Then, very slowly and deliberately, he put the ball on the ground, supported himself on the edge of the lab bench, and stood on it.

"Remarkable," he muttered.

"I thought we could even make football helmets out of that stuff," Joe put in. "Or—you know, if you had a suit made of it, you could take a shower without getting wet."

Dr. Grimes uttered a snarl. "I have listened to quite enough of this nonsense," he burst out. "Bullfinch! I refuse to waste any more time on children's games and toys."

But the Professor wasn't listening. He was staring at Joe, who goggled back at him solemnly.

"Say that again," said the Professor.

"I said," repeated Dr. Grimes irritably, "that I refuse to waste any more—"

"Not you," said the Professor. "I meant Joe. That if we had a suit of this we could shower without getting wet. Was that it?"

Joe nodded silently and somewhat nervously.

"Have you lost your mind, Bullfinch?" Dr. Grimes demanded.

"I don't think so," replied the Professor. "No, I'm sure I haven't. But I may have *found* something."

"Found something?"

"Yes," said the Professor, picking up the football. "The answer to almost all your problems, Grimes."

4
Dr. Grimes's Plans

There was silence for a moment, and then Dr. Grimes's expression slowly changed from annoyance to interest. He looked at the plastic-shelled football in the Professor's hands, and then he said, "I see. You really think there is a possibility—?"

Danny had been gazing in perplexity at the two scientists, and now he said, "Professor, I'm sorry if there's something wrong. It's my fault for telling Joe to throw the ball to me. But you wanted me to get rid of the plastic anyway. . . ."

"There's nothing wrong, my boy," said the Professor. "On the contrary, it may be very right. Sit down, all three of you."

The young people made themselves comfortable, all in a row, on the edge of the lab bench, swinging their legs. Then he went on, "You see, Dr. Grimes is planning a remarkable project for the exploration of the ocean floor. He intends to build a bathyscaphe."

"A what?" Joe interrupted. "A bathtub on skates?"

"Not quite, Joe," laughed Professor Bullfinch. *"Bathy*—from the Greek word for *deep*, and *scaphe* from the word meaning *boat*. A deep-diving submarine in which men can go three or four miles down into the sea. Actually, the word 'submarine' is wrong. It is more like a balloon. But instead of floating up into the air, it floats down into the ocean."

The Professor paused and filled his pipe. Then he continued, "The bathyscaphe was developed by Professor Auguste Piccard, the famous Swiss scientist, about 1948. Before that, Professor William Beebe had made his deep-sea descents in an iron ball called a bathysphere, which was dropped at the end of a steel cable. Professor Piccard's bathyscaphe consists of a ball-shaped cabin underneath a large tank of lightweight gasoline. The gasoline, being lighter than water, makes the ship very buoyant. In order to sink into the sea, heavy ballast, of iron pellets, is taken aboard; the vessel sinks to the bottom; and when its passengers wish to rise, they drop the ballast and float back up to the surface.

"The bathyscaphe has allowed men to go farther down into the ocean than ever was possible before. Professor Piccard, in his vessel the *Trieste,* descended to nearly two miles. Then the French diver, Captain Cousteau, with his companions Huout and Willm, reached a depth of two and a half miles in one called the F.N.R.S. 3. Not long ago, Professor Piccard's son, Jacques, along with a U.S. Navy Lieutenant named Don Walsh, went down seven miles in the *Trieste.*"

"And Dr. Grimes is going to build one of these bathyscaphes?" asked Danny. "Gosh, what an adventure that would be!"

"He has the promise of enough money for the project from the Academy of Scientific Research," said the Professor. "Money has always been the biggest problem. It's hard to make people see the importance of diving into the ocean depths."

"Why?" said Joe. "I should think they'd want to find all that buried treasure that must be lying around down there."

"Trivial!" cried Dr. Grimes, snapping his

fingers. "The thing we must understand is that the sea is our next frontier—just as the old West was a hundred years ago."

"Isn't that what people are always saying about outer space?" asked Irene.

"Yes, my dear," said the Professor. "Men have been working hard to get into outer space, but right here, at our very doorstep, lie uncharted regions that we know almost nothing about. Three-quarters of our earth is under water, yet we know less about some of it than we do about the moon. And in the seas and oceans, and in the rocks and mud at their bottoms, lie oil, precious minerals, and food enough for the whole planet. Why, just think," he exclaimed, his eyes shining with enthusiasm, "almost everything mankind needs is in the sea! Life came out of the sea in the first place! The big job for science now is to go into the depths and study that wonderful world."

Dr. Grimes had been pacing up and down with his hands behind his back. He put in, "I want to build more than a bathyscaphe. I want to build a real undersea laboratory."

"Exactly," the Professor nodded. "You see, when you go down as far as two miles, the pressure of the water is about two and a half tons on every square inch of surface. An ordinary submarine cannot go much farther down than about a thousand feet. Deeper than that, it would be crushed flat. The little round cabin of the present bathyscaphes is very small and made of very strong steel—it's about seven feet in diameter, and its walls are over three inches thick. There isn't much room in it, as you can imagine. What Dr. Grimes wants to build is something with enough space for several men and plenty of equipment. Something shaped like this, for example.''

He tapped the football. ''Ordinary plastics, plexiglass for instance, are not as strong as steel. But this plastic may be what we are looking for.''

''Let's not jump to conclusions,'' said Dr.

Grimes sourly. "We'll have to test it. And what about duplicating the formula?"

"Ah, yes," said the Professor. "Danny, do you think you can remember the temperature at which you reheated it? And how long you let it cool?"

"I think I can remember," Danny said. His eyes were dancing with excitement. "It means that we're really partly the discoverers of the plastic, doesn't it?"

"Well, I imagine it does, in a way," agreed the Professor.

"Then—then maybe we can go with you in the ship you build. Can we, Professor?"

The Professor glanced sidelong at Dr. Grimes. "I must say this certainly changes matters, Grimes. But we have a great deal to do before we have to face that decision. We must get to work at once!"

He clapped his hands together. "A laboratory on the ocean floor. One that can move freely about, like a submarine, but two miles down! What marvelous things are waiting to be discovered, I wonder?"

Danny, Irene, and Joe stared at each other. Then Joe said in a gloomy voice, "I'll bet I know the answer to that, if Danny goes along. Trouble!"

5
The <u>Sea Urchin</u>

Professor Bullfinch had not exaggerated. Many weeks of testing followed, and the two scientists became more and more excited as the properties of the plastic became apparent. It was stronger than any known steel, while at the same time as light and transparent as plexiglass. Experiments showed that a relatively thin shell of it could withstand enormous pressure and yet float like a cork.

In the end, they decided upon making a totally new kind of undersea vessel. Professor Bullfinch explained that they need not follow the design of the bathyscaphe, but instead would combine some of its features with those of a submarine: it would be roughly cigar-shaped, would carry ballast to take it down, and when free of ballast would bob up to the surface again. Unlike a submarine it would have very little machinery, most of its space being arranged for comfortable observation of the sea bottom, and most of its equipment designed to study, photograph, and collect specimens. To help it descend, it would have tanks which could be pumped full of sea water. It would also have small, electrically-driven propellers so that it could move horizontally through the water. In addition, Professor Bullfinch and Dr. Grimes developed some interesting new equipment which they hoped would allow them to gather samples of fish and plants, and the mud and ooze of the ocean floor.

This new vessel, Professor Bullfinch proposed they call a *mesoscaphe*. "The name," he said, "means *middle ship* and was created by Professor Auguste Piccard to describe another type of diving vessel which he considered making. However, it also describes our ship, which is somewhere in the middle between all the other types."

"But we can't simply call it a mesoscaphe," Danny objected. "That sounds like some kind of prehistoric monster. It ought to have a real name."

"Mermaid," suggested Irene.

Dr. Grimes began growling to himself.

"What about *Seafood?*" said Joe.

At this, Dr. Grimes threw down the pencil with which he was making notes and said that unless the laboratory were cleared at once of juvenile visitors, he would leave the project.

"I suggest," said the Professor quietly, "that we table the question of a name until we actually have the ship."

More weeks followed, during which models were built to scale and tested in special tanks in which the pressure was slowly increased until the models exploded. In this way, they were able to calculate the thickness the hull of the mesoscaphe would have to have to endure the thousands of pounds of pressure of the deep. At last, the final plans were approved, and work began on the actual ship. It was decided that Dr. Grimes's original plan of diving in the Pacific Ocean would be followed, and a small town off the western coast of Mexico was chosen as the expedition's base. It was called Nomata.

As Danny said later, it took almost as long to persuade Dr. Grimes that the young people should be allowed to go along, as it did to build the mesoscaphe itself. Even after Dr. Grimes grudgingly agreed that they could come, he refused to consider the possibility of their making any actual dives in the ship. The parents were a little less of a problem; Mrs. Dunn, the Pearsons, and the Millers had a family conference with Professor Bullfinch and the three children. Although Mr. and Mrs. Pearson were at first opposed to the idea of Joe going, Mrs. Dunn persuaded them that it would be a splendid way for the boy to begin learning another language. The Millers had cousins who were planning to vacation in the town of Mazatlán, only a few miles from Nomata, and they promised to drive over and keep an eye on the three, every few days.

The mesoscaphe was to be shipped in the hold of a freighter by way of the Panama Canal, and it was decided that the two scientists and the three young people would travel by the same ship. With them would go the man who had been chosen to pilot the undersea laboratory, a famous English diver and submarine captain named Reginald Beaversmith.

Captain Beaversmith was a tall, untidy man, whose bronzed face was crisscrossed with tiny wrinkles from sun and wind. He had seen much action at sea during the war and later had learned skin diving from the noted French diver, Captain Cousteau, in the Mediterranean. When the whole group had at last begun the voyage, on a freighter called the S.S. *Acapulco* just one year after the discovery of the wonderful plastic, he passed many days with the three young people, sitting on deck in the sun and telling them stories of his adventures.

On one such day, they were sitting together up near the bow of the ship, Captain Beaversmith on a winch, and Danny, Joe, and Irene sprawled on deck. They had passed through the Panama Canal the day before. The fresh wind whipped spray over them from time to time, and all about them wheeled the blue waters of the Pacific. The Captain was saying, "It was a day very much like this. We surfaced near the islands, and there, anchored just off the reef was a Japanese destroyer. . . ." He stopped, scratched his chin, and chuckled. "Sorry, chaps," he said. "Does this sound vaguely familiar? I have a feeling that I may have told it to you before."

"We don't know yet," said Danny. "Go on."

"Yes, well, one war story is very much like another, you know. That's the trouble. They seem to rush together and blend into one story, sometimes. 'So may a thousand actions, once afoot, End in one purpose. . . .' Shakespeare."

"Gee, you know a lot of poetry," said Joe enviously.

"One of the few advantages of an English public school education," said the Captain. "They encourage you to look at poetry."

"Have you ever written any yourself?" Danny asked.

"Alas, no. All I can do is quote other people's."

"Joe's going to be a writer when he grows up," Irene said. "You ought to hear some of his poetry."

"I should like that very much," said the Captain courteously.

But just at that moment Professor Bullfinch came forward, shading his eyes with his hand. "Captain Beaversmith," he called. "I'm sorry to interrupt you, but I wonder if you'd come down into the hold with us."

"Certainly, Professor." The Captain got to his feet. "Is anything wrong?"

"Oh, no. But Dr. Grimes and I want to inspect the mesoscaphe. We'll be in Nomata tomorrow, and we want to make a last checkup."

"Can we come, too, Professor?" Danny cried, springing up.

"Yes, of course. Dr. Grimes is waiting for us below."

He led the way to the hold. The *Acapulco* had a very large hold in the center of the ship, designed to carry machinery and automobiles, and into this the mesoscaphe was fitted, carefully held in a wooden cradle and lashed down with cables. In the gloomy hold it looked like a fairy ship, its plastic sides gleaming like glass. It seemed much too fragile to carry men to the sea bottom.

A rope ladder dangled down its side from the conning tower, for, like a tiny submarine, it had a deck and a conning tower with a hatch. The Professor clambered nimbly up the ladder, followed by Captain Beaversmith and the three children. There was a metal ladder inside the conning tower, and they climbed down this into the little cabin. Through the transparent hull of the undersea laboratory, they could see the walls of the hold, lighted by a couple of bare electric bulbs.

"Golly," said Joe, "are you sure this plastic will really keep the water out?"

"We have estimated," said the Professor, "that the three-inch-thick shell will resist a pressure of nearly ten tons to the square inch."

"I hope you estimated right," Joe mumbled. "It would be a shame to get down to the bottom and find that you were wrong by a couple of zeros."

"If it's so light in weight, though," said Irene, "what will make it sink to the bottom?"

"In the first place," said the Captain, "we'll

have two batteries fastened on deck to give us our electric lights. Each one weighs thirteen hundred pounds. There are other batteries in the ship to power the motors. We will also carry about a ton of ballast in the form of lead pellets, or shot. And we have tanks fore and aft, on both sides of the ship—you can see them better from the outside as bulges in the hull. Those can be pumped full of sea water. All this weight will take us down. Then, when we want to shoot back to the surface, we blow the tanks—that is, pump out the sea water— drop the shot, and ditch our batteries, and up she rises, 'earlye in the morning,' as the old song has it.''

He was interrupted by a roaring sound and a loud yell from the after part of the cabin. Everyone turned in alarm. Danny was clinging to the side of a big square tank, and his hair was blowing straight out as if from a large electric fan. Captain Beaversmith made his way as quickly as he could to the spot and seized a small wheel. He gave it a half turn and then pushed a lever. The roaring stopped.

Danny smoothed down his hair. ''What— what happened?'' he gasped.

''We might ask the same thing,'' said Dr. Grimes sternly. ''You've only been in the ship

40

five minutes, young man, and you're already beginning to wreck her.''

"Not quite as bad as that," said the Professor. "And I'm sure it was an accident."

"I was only looking into this tank," Danny said, "just to see what it was, and my foot slipped. I grabbed that lever to hold myself steady. Next thing I knew, a hurricane started to blow on me from the tank."

"Ah, that's our suction pump intake," said the Professor. "You see, that long tube connects with an intake valve outside the hull. When we want to take in any interesting specimens, we manipulate the hose just like a— well, a vacuum cleaner. It has a new type of motor that creates a powerful suction, and it sucks the specimens into this tank, along with sea water so they can be kept alive. Of course, there's no water outside now, so nothing but air came in. But really, Dan, you'd better try not to touch anything else."

"Here are the grab-arms," said Captain Beaversmith, motioning to what looked like a pair of metal sleeves hanging from rods in the ceiling. "Another wonderful collecting device, I must say. These are fastened to jointed arms outside the hull, with claws on the ends of them. By putting your arms in the sleeves, you

41

can move the outside claws to pick things up. They can then be brought inside through an air lock."

"Everything is just as we planned it," beamed the Professor, "the air-purification system, the remote-control searchlights, all the instruments. I suggest we work over the ship from stem to stern, Captain Beaversmith, and make sure everything is in order so the meso-scaphe can be put in the water tomorrow when we arrive."

"Then perhaps the urchins had better leave," said the Captain. "It is a trifle crowded with six of us in the cabin."

"Urchins?" said Joe. "Who are they?"

"Us, silly," said Irene. "Urchins means kids. You'd better learn some more words if you plan to be a writer. Coming, Danny?"

Danny was staring absent-mindedly into space. He said, "Wait a sec. I've got an idea—"

"Oh-oh," groaned Joe.

"No ideas here, please, Dan," said the Professor warningly.

"This is just an idea for a name for the ship," Danny protested. "How about *Sea Urchin?*"

"Not bad," said Captain Beaversmith. "But a sea urchin is also a round, prickly little creature, and the mesoscaphe is cigar-shaped and smooth. I'm afraid it won't do.''

"Sure it will," Joe snickered. "Professor Bullfinch is round. And Dr. Grimes is prickly. It just fits.''

Dr. Grimes drew himself up, frowning. But the Professor burst into laughter and clapped Danny on the shoulder. ''And you three are

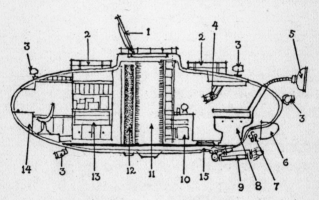

Cross section of the Sea Urchin

1. HATCH COVER (open)
2. BATTERIES
3. SEARCHLIGHTS
4. SLEEVES
5. SUCTION INTAKE
6. RUDDER
7. PROPELLER
8. COLLECTING TANK
9. GRAB ARMS
10. LABORATORY BENCH
11. SHOT BALLAST TANK
12. CORE SAMPLER
13. FOOD, WATER AND SUPPLIES
14. PILOT'S CONTROL SECTION
15. AIR LOCK

certainly urchins," he cried. "An excellent name." He beamed round at the others. "Let us get to work at once. And when we are done, we'll all meet in the dining room and drink a toast to success—to the *Sea Urchin,* long may she happily dive!"

6
Trial Dive

Professor Bullfinch rubbed his hands, looking about the sunny public square of Nomata. Behind him rose the pink stucco front of their hotel, the Hotel Grande, and beyond, between the trunks of feathery coconut palms, could be glimpsed the deep blue of the Pacific. An air of sleepiness and tranquillity hung over the red tile roofs of the town.

"Delightful," he said. "We should be very comfortable here."

Dr. Grimes scowled. "Please remember, Bullfinch," he said, "that we are here to work. We did not choose this locality for comfort, but because of the variety and quantity of marine life in this area."

"You mean we can't have any fun at all?" Danny asked sadly.

"Fun?" said Dr. Grimes, as if he had found a fly swimming in his soup. "I wish I had never listened to Bullfinch, but had insisted on leaving you all home. However, since you might possibly be considered co-discoverers of the plastic, and your parents were foolish enough to let you come, bear in mind that your basic duty will be to keep out of the way and not interfere with work."

"That's easy," said Joe. "I just love not interfering with work."

The Professor cleared his throat. "I suggest," he put in, "that we go to the waterfront. Captain Beaversmith must have the *Sea Urchin* ready by now."

They set off down the single, paved main street, between rows of neat adobe houses painted in soft pinks, yellows, and creamy whites. The street opened onto a wide road that skirted the edge of the curving bay. White sand and dark boulders ran down to the water, and on either side of the bay huge rocks, their bases girdled with white foam, guarded the entrance. Fishermen's huts lined the shore, and there were nets everywhere stretched on wooden frames, drying in the sun.

When they came out on the beach they found

quite a crowd collected at one point. "I'll bet that's the *Sea Urchin*," Danny said. "They've never seen anything like her."

He was right. The glistening little vessel bobbed in the shallows, reflecting the bright sun as if she were made of gold. Most of the town had turned out to stare at the strange sight: there were women in black dresses, fishermen in dirty white-duck pants and broad-brimmed straw hats, and even businessmen and merchants who had deserted their shops and offices to stare and point and chatter and take photographs.

Dr. Grimes and the Professor pushed their way through the crowd. They found Captain Beaversmith standing barefoot in the surf, deep in talk with a brown old fisherman. When he caught sight of them, he smiled and waved.

"Welcome to the fiesta!" he shouted.

"How is everything?" said the Professor.

"Smashing!" the Captain replied.

"What—broken to bits?" said Joe. "I knew there'd be trouble."

"No, no, simply an expression," chuckled the Captain. "Means tiptop shape. I've just arranged with El Bagre, here, to rent his rowboat as a daily taxi to the *Urchin*."

The fisherman nodded and smiled, his white teeth shining in his leathery face. A plump,

"My uncle is proud that you choose his boat."

moon-faced boy of about Danny's age stood beside him. This boy said, "My uncle does not speak very much English, so I will be the translator. He is very proud that you choose his boat."

"Good show," said the Captain. "Here, you urchins, this is Ramon. He's been helping out this morning, getting things shipshape."

"Hello," said Danny, putting out his hand.

"I am pleased to meet you," Ramon said gravely, shaking hands first with Danny, then with Joe and Irene.

"Is your last name Bagre, too, like your uncle's?" Danny asked.

Ramon's face split in a grin. "We are not named Bagre. He is called *El Bagre*—that means a catfish—because of his whiskers. Our name is Almazan."

"Well, gentlemen, are you ready for the trial dive?" Captain Beaversmith was saying to the two scientists.

"I'm looking forward to it," said Professor Bullfinch.

" 'A man he seems of cheerful yesterdays and confident tomorrows,' " smiled the Captain. "Wordsworth. Very well, then, into the boat. El Bagre will row us out."

"You three young people will wait for us on the beach," said the Professor. "Irene, your mother's relatives will be here at noon to visit you, so please be sure you don't vanish. I rely on you to keep an eye on the boys.''

The Captain helped the Professor and Dr. Grimes into the rowboat, and they went out to the *Urchin*. They climbed aboard, the hatch was closed, and El Bagre brought his boat back to shore. Very slowly, the *Sea Urchin* began to move out into the bay. When she was half-way out, where the bottom dropped to nearly eight fathoms, or about forty-eight feet, she began to descend. The sunlight winked from her hull, and then, suddenly, she was gone.

The dive was planned to last half an hour, and the three friends and Ramon sat down on the sand to wait.

7
Food for Thought

"Gosh, I wonder what they're seeing now," Danny said wistfully, poking holes in the damp sand with his finger. "All sorts of wonderful things, I'll bet. Maybe sunken treasure, or strange fish. . . ."

"Or mermaids," giggled Irene.

"Oh, be serious."

"I am serious. You know what the Professor told us: scientists still don't know much about the sea. For all we know maybe there *are* mermaids."

Joe had been sitting with his back against a warm rock. He said lazily, "I wonder, if they found mermaids, how they'd count them—as fish or people? Because, if they were fish, you could eat them, and if they were people, they'd have to vote."

Danny took a long breath of the salty air. "Mmm," he said. "It sure smells good. I wish we could go down to the bottom with them in the *Urchin*. If only Dr. Grimes weren't such a grouch."

"We'll have plenty to do anyway," Irene said comfortingly. "There's the countryside and the town to explore, and we can swim, and Captain Beaversmith has promised to teach us skin diving. . . . Golly, doesn't it make you feel all tingly with excitement?"

Joe squinted up at the sun. "It must be nearly noon," he said. "You know how that makes me feel?"

"How?"

"Hungry." He glanced at Ramon, who had been squatting, listening to them with a solemn expression on his face. "You look like a boy who enjoys eating. Maybe you can steer me to some good local dishes?"

"Oh, you like to eat?" said Ramon. "I do, too. Maybe we can trade, eh? Did you bring some American *delicadeza*—something tasty?"

Joe scrambled to his feet. "Sure," he replied. "I always carry emergency rations with me. I've got some up at the hotel. I'll get them, and you go home and get some interesting things to eat, and we'll meet back here. Okay?''

"Interesting?" Ramon raised his eyebrows. "That's what you like? *Seguramente!* That means okay.''

It took only a few minutes for the two to run their errands. Joe came panting back with a paper bag, and a moment or two later Ramon trotted along the sand with a basket on his arm.

"A couple of experimental scientists," Danny snickered, rolling over and sitting up. "I hope you two will be very happy together."

"Oh, I'd love to try some of Ramon's delicacies," Irene said. "May I?"

"Of course," said Ramon. He sat down and began fishing in the contents of his basket.

Joe opened his bag and brought out a somewhat sticky roll of candy with a silver paper wrapper. "Here," he said. "Try mine first."

Ramon took it gingerly and peeled off the wrapper. "It looks like mud with little stones in it," he said.

"It kind of melted a little," Joe admitted. "It's good, though. It's called a Munchy Chew Bar."

Ramon began reading what was written on the wrapper. "It says," he muttered, "that it contains cocoa, powdered milk, lecithin, peanuts, vanillin, and artificial flavor. It doesn't sound very nice. What is this lecithin?''

"I don't know," said Joe, "but lots of candy has it, so it must be good."

Ramon took a cautious bite. "Ook!" he said. "I eef uck oo evver."

"What?" said Joe. "What's the matter?"

"He says his teeth are stuck together," Danny translated. "Keep working on it, Ramon. It'll just let go all of a sudden, and you'll be able to talk again."

Ramon managed to free his teeth. *"No me gusta,"* he said firmly. "I don't like it."

"Well," said Joe, "it just takes a little getting used to. Like olives, you know. You don't like the taste of them at first, and then you get used to them. Let me try one of your dishes, now."

Ramon took out a clay bowl in which were small bits of some sort of green vegetable. Cautiously, Joe took a taste.

"It's kind of odd," he said swallowing. "A sort of pale-green flavor. What is it?"

"Nopalitos," said Ramon. "Cactus."

"Cactus?" Joe turned pale. "Oh my gosh! I can feel the spikes sticking into my stomach already."

"Don't be silly, Joe," said Irene, calmly.

She had taken some of the vegetable, too, as had Danny. "There aren't any spikes. It's pretty good, in fact."

"A scientist should be open-minded," Danny said severely, "and should experiment with new things. That's what Professor Bullfinch always says. This isn't bad at all. It tastes a little like asparagus."

Joe opened his bag again. "All right," he said to Ramon. "Try this."

He held out a small brown square. "These are root-beer drops. Not everybody likes them, but I think they're refreshing."

Ramon licked his lips. Then, reluctantly, he took the candy, unwrapped it, and popped it into his mouth. He smiled broadly. "Ah-h-h," he said. "That is *something* to eat. *Gracias, José.*"

He reached into his basket and took out a large gray pancake rolled up around something. "This is a *tortilla*," he said. "It is a corn-meal pancake, and we use them like bread." He unrolled it. Inside were some strips of what looked like bicycle tire, grayish-white and rubbery.

Joe hesitated for a moment. At last he took a piece and bit into it. "Hey, not bad," he said.

The other two tried it, and Irene said, "It's

chewy, isn't it? Is it a kind of fish, Ramon?"

"Yes," Ramon nodded. "That is *pulpo*. You know, the one that swims backward, with eight arms. . . ."

"Eight a-a-arms?" Joe stammered.

Danny gulped. "Suddenly I don't feel very scientific," he said. "I have a kind of feeling that what he means is octopus."

"That's right. Octopus," Ramon smiled. "You said you wanted something interesting."

"I don't know what you boys are being so squirmy about," Irene said cheerfully. "It's good. What's the difference whether it has eight arms or no arms? You eat oysters, don't you? And clams?"

"You must develop a taste for it," Ramon said slyly. "Like Munchy Chewy Bar, no?"

"That's right," Joe muttered. "NO!"

Fortunately, just then, Danny jumped up and pointed out to sea, shading his eyes. "Look, it's the *Urchin*," he said. "She's surfaced."

The others turned to stare. The little ship had appeared, far out in the bay, and as they watched it began to move slowly toward the shore.

"Gosh, I wonder what they brought back?" Danny breathed.

"Maybe they found the treasure of Montezuma," Ramon said with a broad grin.

"Treasure? What treasure?" Danny demanded.

Ramon cocked an eye at him. "You don't know? I thought that was one of the reasons your friends went out in the little glass boat."

"Never heard of it," Joe said. "What's the story?"

"Why, everyone around here knows of it," said Ramon with a mysterious air. "You see, many hundreds of years ago the great king Montezuma fought with the Spanish invaders, led by Hernando Cortez. Cortez defeated the Aztecs and killed Montezuma, and when this happened the priests of the great Sun Temple took the golden image of the sun and ran away with it to the coast. They started to sail to Baja California, but a great storm arose and their boat was sunk."

He shrugged. "Many men have searched for it, but they don't know where it lies."

"Do you?" Danny said.

Ramon stuck out his lower lip. "Maybe," he said, half closing his eyes. "Maybe I do and maybe I don't."

People were running down the beach, and the *Sea Urchin* came gliding into the shallows. Captain Beaversmith climbed out of the conning tower and ran forward to let the anchor go. Ramon's uncle, El Bagre, rowed out and in a very short time the Captain, Dr. Grimes, and Professor Bullfinch were on the beach. The young people ran to meet them.

"How did it go, Professor?" Danny cried.

"Did you find the treasure?" yelled Joe.

"Amazing, truly amazing," said the Professor, beaming at the cheering crowd. "What? Treasure? No, we collected nothing, Joe. This was only a trial."

"And she handles like a dream," said Captain Beaversmith jovially. "Like piloting a rocking-horse. Why don't we take the nippers out tomorrow for a ride?"

"Absolutely not," said Dr. Grimes firmly. "I will not have children messing about with our work."

"But gosh, Dr. Grimes," said Joe, "There's a buried treasure out there somewhere. A golden image of the sun—!"

"Ridiculous!" Dr. Grimes snapped. "The only treasure out there is to be found in the samples I intend to take from the floor of the ocean: radioactive ores, perhaps, or oil. You three will remain on shore."

"Let's not make hasty decisions," smiled Professor Bullfinch. "We'll see how things go. Come, Grimes, we must develop the pictures we took."

He set off for the hotel. Danny and Irene

turned to follow, but Joe remained staring out at the sea.

"Hey, Joe, come on," said Danny.

"A golden image of the sun," Joe said. "How about that? We'd be rich for life. I'd give anything if I could find out where it is."

Ramon looked at him. "Anything? Would you give all the rest of those drops of root beer?"

Joe snorted. "Well, sure!"

"Joe!" Danny said. "Let's go. So long, Ramon. See you soon."

He pulled his friend by the arm. Ramon looked after them, nodding. "All the root beer drops, eh? Maybe I can arrange it," he murmured.

8
The Treasure Map

Danny was dreaming of the sea. In his dream he was swimming slowly beside a mermaid. Out of the depths a fish appeared holding a golden disk—an Aztec image of the sun. Danny was paralyzed. Closer and closer came the fish, grinning and gaping as he lighted his way with the sun image. "Hey!" Danny cried. "That's hot! Get away from me!" The fish drew closer, and Danny's face grew warmer, and suddenly he awoke with a strangled yell.

A bright beam of sunlight was coming through the Venetian blinds of the hotel bedroom window and striking right on his nose. He rubbed his eyes and yawned and jumped out of bed. He pulled up the blind and stepped out on the balcony. The sun blazed down upon the square; a few automobiles went by with a squealing of tires; and a seller of pumpkin seeds slowly pushed his cart into the shade.

"Boy, what a country!" Danny whispered. "We've been here for nine days now, and every day is brighter than the one before."

He dragged Joe out of bed, complaining and wailing, and they put on their swimming trunks and light shirts. Then they went to meet Irene who was already up, dressed in a bathing suit and shirt, and leaning over her own balcony watching the square. They went down to the dining room and Danny, who had been practicing Spanish, ordered *huevos fritos con jamon* with a great air of nonchalance.

The young people were busily eating their ham and eggs when the two scientists and Captain Beaversmith came in.

Professor Bullfinch blinked at Danny's plate. "Hmmm," he said. "Don't you think you ought to learn the Spanish words for some other kind of breakfast, Dan?"

"But I like ham and eggs," Danny protested.

"I've been learning all kinds of words from reading the signs on shops," said Joe. "The only trouble is I never get a chance to use those words when I'm talking to anybody."

"What kind of words?" asked Dr. Grimes, tucking his napkin under his chin.

"Oh, for instance, *plomero,* or *ferretería*—those are 'plumber' and 'hardware.' And I learned a good one yesterday—*fabricante de dentaduras.*"

He sighed and shook his head. "But I don't know how I can ever get that into a conversation with Ramon."

"Why? What does it mean?" asked Professor Bullfinch.

"Maker of false teeth," said Joe mournfully.

Captain Beaversmith laughed. "Very simple, my lad. You're always discussing food with Ramon, aren't you? You simply say, in Spanish, 'Ramon, let us not eat so many sweets, or we will have to go to the maker of false teeth.' "

"Yes," added Professor Bullfinch with a chuckle, "and you can also say, 'My stomach feels peculiar; I shall have to find a plumber.' "

Dr. Grimes broke in, "I don't wish to put a stop to all your merriment, but I'd like to remind you that we plan to make a deep dive this morning. Are we almost ready?"

"How far down are you going, Professor?" Danny said.

"We hope to get to seven hundred fathoms," Professor Bullfinch answered. "That's nearly a mile. And what are you young people planning?"

"I'm going to gather shells for my collection," said Irene.

"I'm working on a poem," Joe said.

"Well," said Danny, "I'm going to try to record the sounds of starfish."

The Professor raised his eyebrows. "Starfish? Do they make any sounds?"

"I don't know," said Danny. "That's what I'm going to find out."

"Yesterday he tried to get the sounds of crabs. He kept following one little crab around for an hour, but it wouldn't talk to him," said Joe.

"Maybe it was just sulky," Irene said.

"Maybe crabs don't make any sounds," said Captain Beaversmith.

"Well, a scientist mustn't be discouraged," Danny said stoutly, "I haven't had much luck so far, but I'm going to keep trying."

They finished breakfast, and then they all went off to the shore. The three men were rowed out to the *Sea Urchin;* Irene took her collecting basket and went strolling along the beach, while Joe settled himself comfortably with his back against a heap of sand so that he could think better. Danny took his tape recorder and began searching the rock pools near one arm of the bay. Professor Bullfinch's friend, Dr. Brenton, had loaned the boy a hydrophone, a special underwater microphone with great sensitivity, and he had waterproofed his tape recorder so that he could continue his attempts to record the sounds of fish. The pools were full of starfish of all sorts—some with spotted or striped arms, some with many slender arms like little snakes—and he faithfully held his microphone near all of them. But at last he was forced to admit to himself that either his microphone wasn't quite sensitive enough, or else starfish didn't make sounds, either.

"Or else, they just don't feel like talking," he thought sadly, as he walked back up the beach to join the others. "After all, I feel that way myself, sometimes, so why shouldn't they?"

He woke Joe, and they went in for a swim together, and a short time later Irene joined them with her basket of shells. They were inspecting her finds when Ramon came up.

"Olé, amigos," he called. "How are you this morning?"

"Fine," Danny said. "We're waiting for the *Sea Urchin*. It should be coming back any minute now."

Ramon turned to Joe. "Have you still got some drops of root beer, José?"

"Sure," said Joe. "Lots of them. Why?"

Ramon squatted down on the sand. "Don't you remember, you said you would give all the rest of them if you could find out where the treasure of the Aztecs lies?"

Joe sat up straight. "Have you got a map?"

Ramon nodded.

"Let's see it," said Danny.

Ramon reached into the front of his shirt and brought out a folded piece of what looked like parchment.

"Where'd you get it?" Joe demanded.

"From my uncle, El Bagre. I told him what you wanted. First, he laughed a long time. Then he was very solemn. Then he went into the shed, and when he came out he gave me this."

Danny reached for it. "Wait," said Ramon. "First, the drops."

"You can trust Joe," Danny said. "If this is really a map showing where the treasure is, we'll see to it he gives you the candy."

He took the map. "Feels like old parchment, all right," he said.

The other two crowded close, holding their breath. Slowly, he unfolded it. Then his mouth fell open in astonishment.

The piece of parchment was perfectly blank, except for a small cross in the very center and two words. The words were *Oceano Pacifico*.

"The cross," said Ramon, "is where the treasure lies."

"Hey, now wait a minute," Joe spluttered. "In the middle of the Pacific Ocean? We knew that!"

Ramon looked hurt. "I cannot help that," he said. "You said that you would give anything for a map showing where the treasure is."

"But—" said Joe.

"My uncle said that this is a true map of where the treasure is."

"But—"

"A bargain is a bargain. No?"

"But—but—"

"I'm afraid he's right, Joe," said Danny, somewhere between laughter and disappointment. "You owe him the root-beer drops."

"Okay," said Joe bitterly. "I know when I'm licked. I'm going to keep this map, though. Someday, I just might be in the middle of the ocean. . . . I never did like root-beer drops," he added, getting to his feet. "I prefer octopus, any day!"

9
The Language of Fish

When the *Sea Urchin* came back to the surface from its seven-hundred-fathom dive, it brought such interesting specimens in its collecting tanks that they almost made up for the disappointment of the treasure map.

The three young people were allowed to come on board after the ship had anchored. The deck of the cabin was wet, and there was a fishy, salty smell in the air. Every inch of space was full of jars and tubs in which were sea cucumbers, starfish, anemones, larval shrimp, fish, and shellfish of all sorts.

"But come and look at these," said the Professor proudly. "Here are the real prizes of the dive."

He led the three children to the big collecting
tank, which was attached to the suction pump
in the after end of the cabin. Its compartments
were now filled with sea water, and as the
young people bent over them they saw in the
first one some flashes of pale light.

"Fireflies!" said Joe. "Water fireflies?"

The Professor laughed. "Firefishes would be
more accurate."

He snapped on a light above the tank. They
could see, now, that in the compartment were
a number of fish no more than two or three
inches long. They had large, sad, wide-open
mouths, bulging eyes, and flat, almost transparent bodies. Along their sides and bellies

were shimmering pink lights that made the water of the tank glow.

"They are a variety of *Argyropelecus,* or hatchetfish," the Professor explained. "We found this type a good deal farther down than is usual."

"And the lights help them find their way around, is that it?" asked Danny.

The Professor tapped his teeth with his pipe-stem. "Well, we're not sure what the lights do," he replied. "Perhaps they attract food. There are several theories, but no one really knows. They aren't the only luminous fish in the depths. Look here."

He pointed into the second compartment. Three fairly large fish, over a foot long, swam in it. They were snaky-looking, and their heads had round staring eyes and large mouths, with oversized curved teeth. Like the hatchetfish, their skin was transparent and even their teeth were like cloudy glass. Their sides were studded with beautiful glowing lights, like the port-holes of a ship at night.

"Chauliodus," said the Professor. "A variety of viperfish."

"Whew! I wouldn't like to have half a dozen of those things coming after me," said Joe.

"Oh, I don't think you need worry. They

live deep in the sea, and they're more interested in eating hatchetfish than boys."

Danny had brought along his tape recorder. He said, "Please, Professor, can I try to make some recordings of them?"

"I don't see why not," Professor Bullfinch said. "I don't think they make any audible sound, however."

"Still trying for the language of fish, eh?" Dr. Grimes said. He joined them at the tank, wiping preserving fluid from his hands with a towel.

"Plong," said Danny. Carefully, he lowered the hydrophone into the tank full of hatchetfish.

"I beg your pardon," said Dr. Grimes. "Did you say, 'wrong'?"

"Plong," said Irene. "It means yes, in fish talk."

"What? Fish talk?" Both Dr. Grimes and the Professor stared at her.

"Oh, not in real fish language," Irene hastened to add. "We've made up our own secret language out of the sounds of different fish. We use it once in a while for fun."

"Beware!" said Captain Beaversmith, coming up behind them. "If you talk like a fish, you may grow to look like a fish. How does it go?

'Full fathom five thy father lies;
Of his bones are coral made;
Those are pearls that were his eyes;
Nothing of him that doth fade
But doth suffer a sea change. . . .' ''

"Shakespeare?" said Joe.

"Yes. 'The Tempest.' ''

"Ha!" Joe exclaimed. "I can hear poems from May to December, But poets' names I can't remember."

"Who wrote that?" chuckled the Captain.

"Me," said Joe cheerfully.

"You mean 'I,' '' said Irene primly.

"Chirk," said Joe. "Which in fish talk means, 'Oh, for goodness' sake, do you always have to correct me?' ''

Danny pulled up the hydrophone, rewound the tape a little way, and turned the recorder switch on. He started it, and from the amplifier came a series of faint cheeps, like small sleepy birds.

"Great heavens!" exclaimed the Professor. "Remarkable! You have actually recorded some sounds of this particular *Argyropelecus*. Grimes, this is splendid, a real contribution to the work of our expedition. Don't you agree?"

Dr. Grimes nodded reluctantly. "Very interesting, certainly," he said.

Danny shot a quick glance at Irene. Then he said innocently, "Do you really think it's important, Dr. Grimes?"

"Well, I—" Dr. Grimes began, but the Professor interrupted him.

"Every bit of information we can acquire about the sea is important," he said. "We may not understand its value right now, but it will have importance someday. For instance, when Professor Piccard made his first balloon flight into the stratosphere, many people could not understand its use. Today, however, with flights into the stratosphere almost commonplace, we recognize the value of his investigations in the development of high-altitude aviation and space flight."

"I see," said Danny slowly. "Then, don't you think it would be a good thing if I took my recording machine down on the next deep dive you make?"

Professor Bullfinch snorted with amusement, and Captain Beaversmith roared with laughter. "You might have a little trouble getting outside the ship to make recordings," said the Professor. "But I can recognize a good strong hint when I hear one. You all want to go down with us, don't you?"

"It's impossible," snapped Dr. Grimes.

The Professor raised his eyebrows. "My dear Grimes, nothing is impossible," he said. "Some things are just harder to believe than others."

Dr. Grimes tightened his lips. "I will not have children fooling about with the serious affairs of science," he said.

"Tut, tut!" the Professor smiled. "Is this 'Snapper' Grimes I hear talking? The same person who at the age of fourteen wrote a paper on the binary system which made his science teacher furious? And didn't that teacher say to you, at that time, that children shouldn't fool about with the serious affairs of science?"

Dr. Grimes's cheeks turned red. The Professor quietly lit his pipe. And Captain Beaversmith, running his fingers through his unkempt hair, said, "As a matter of fact, I don't see why the kids shouldn't have a go. They've been jolly good sports so far, and they have behaved well. I say, let 'em come along tomorrow—not for a deep 'un, but down to a couple of hundred fathoms. As far as the ship is concerned, we've seen for ourselves how safe it is."

Professor Bullfinch nodded his agreement. The three young people looked at Dr. Grimes and waited.

At last Dr. Grimes said, "Very well. But remember, Bullfinch, if Danny acts in a head-strong way or makes any trouble, I'll hold you personally responsible."

"I'm not afraid of responsibility," said the Professor quietly. "I think you know that already."

10
Into the Depths

The *Sea Urchin* sailed between the jagged rocky headlands of Puerta Nomata bay and then began her dive. To the three young people crowded close to one of the transparent sides of the hull, it was a breathtaking sight to see the water slowly rise past their faces until the blue-green sea had closed over their heads.

The sunlight was not yet cut off. It made the water bright and clear as crystal, and twinkled upon millions of tiny floating specks, like starry dust, only they were alive—microscopic plants and animals. Their sky was now a shining but hazy mirror. There was no feeling of movement; it was only by seeing the fish or plants move past that they could judge they were descending. There was almost no sound in the ship except for the hum of electric motors and the clicking of the pressure recorder. In this quiet they moved steadily forward and downward, and the water slowly darkened about them.

"Gosh, it's pretty," said Danny.

"Pretty?" said Irene. "Isn't that just like a boy? It's *beautiful!*"

"Yes, and it makes me nervous, too," said Joe. "I smell trouble. Suppose something goes wrong, and we can't get back up?"

"Oh, Joe, relax," Danny said, slapping his friend's back. "It's as safe as riding a bicycle."

"Is that so? Well, I once fell off a bicycle and sprained my wrist, and skinned my nose, and broke a cellar window," said Joe. "How safe is that?"

"Nobody else is worried," Danny said. "There isn't going to be any trouble."

He turned away from the side of the hull and began to walk toward the front of the cabin, still staring out at the water. His foot caught in something on the floor, and he uttered a yell and fell headlong.

"Ah-HA!" said Joe triumphantly. "No trouble, eh? I think I'll get out and walk home."

Danny picked himself up, rubbing his knees and wincing. Professor Bullfinch hastened to him and said, "Are you all right?"

"I'm okay," said Danny. "But I stumbled over something—" He looked down and pointed. "There are four eyebolts in the floor here. I never noticed them. That's what tripped me."

He glanced at the ceiling. "And there are four hooks up there. What are they for?"

The Professor looked a bit embarrassed. "Oh—why—hum! I'm sorry you stumbled, my boy. Those hooks? Why, they're—well, I'll explain them another time. You're sure you aren't hurt?"

"I'm sure," said Danny, looking a little surprised, for it wasn't like the Professor to be so evasive.

Just then Irene let out a shout. "My gracious, Professor, come here, quick! It's a sea monster!"

They all rushed to the side. Through the plastic, they could see what looked like a gigantic ball covered with spikes. It was almost as tall as one of the children, and as it floated nearer to the ship it turned a round eye the size of a saucer on them.

"It's a puffer fish," said Dr. Grimes, coming up beside them. "But it's ten times normal size."

As they watched, the round fish swelled up even larger so that the sharp spikes with which

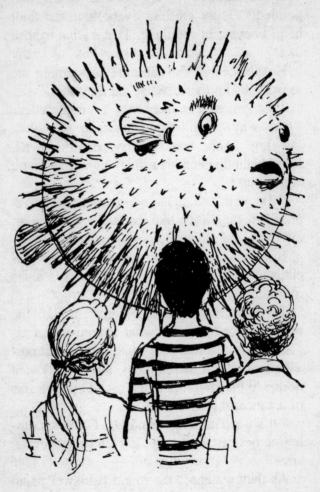

Irene let out a shout, "It's a sea monster."

its body was covered stood out on every side. Then it seemed to see the watchers in the ship, and suddenly it flattened like a deflated football and swam swiftly away.

"We've noticed the unusual size of many fish in these waters," the Professor remarked. "The Beaudette Foundation's expedition found that there was some quality in a strip of water along this coast which made fish and seaweed grow to an amazing degree. What's more, the fish were remarkably healthy and free from disease. It would be wonderful if we could find the reason—a real benefit to mankind."

"How big do the fish grow?" asked Irene.

"Well, the Beaudette Foundation noted that yellowtails, which weigh about twenty pounds when caught off San Diego, can be found weighing nearly a hundred pounds off Central America. Only a few days ago, Dr. Grimes spotted a marlin which must have weighed half a ton. They usually weigh around two hundred pounds."

"Suppose we meet a whale that's grown to ten times its normal size," said Joe in a hollow voice. "And suppose it thinks we're a sardine."

"Let's face that when it happens, Joe," said the Professor. "Look how blue the water's getting. What's our depth, Captain?"

Captain Beaversmith, seated at the controls up forward, glanced at the depth gauge. "Three hundred and fifty feet. We're below the level of safe aqualung diving."

All the reds and yellows of the spectrum had been filtered out of the water by the depth, and its color was a deep blue like that of an evening sky. The Professor switched on the four bright spotlights outside the hull; they were controlled from inside so that they could be turned in any direction. The water was very clear, and once in a while brightly colored fish would swim into the circle of their lights as if to examine them, and then would flick away again. Once, a brilliant golden fish with blue spots moved up alongside them; it was fully six feet long.

"Biggest goldfish I ever saw," said Joe.

"It's a skipjack," the Professor said. "They are rarely more than two feet long. Delicious eating."

He broke off. The skipjack had vanished as he spoke, and the water began to grow cloudy. In a few moments, they appeared to be moving through a cloud of small bugs.

"Five hundred feet," announced Captain Beaversmith. "We're in the soup."

Joe clutched at Danny. "I knew it. Now the trouble starts."

"Why?" asked Dan.

"You heard the Captain. We're in the soup."

Irene had her face pressed to the side of the hull. "He's right," she said. "It *is* like soup."

The boys gazed through the transparent sides. All about them, the searchlights showed a mass of small luminous particles, and looking closer they could see that these were alive: there were tiny shrimps, jellyfish, and many other creatures, most of them no bigger than pinheads.

"Speaking of eating—and of whales," said the Professor, looking over their shoulders, "this 'soup' is called plankton, and it is what the larger whales eat. If it keeps them healthy, you can imagine how nourishing it is. Plankton may very well be one of the answers to the world's food problems."

"Yes, but how does it taste?" Joe said.

"Why not try some?" suggested the Professor. "We want to take some samples anyway."

He went to the collecting tank, which had been emptied in preparation for the trip, and pressed the button that started the suction in-take. They could dimly see the nozzle, which looked a good deal like the nozzle of a vacuum cleaner, stretch out beyond the rear of the hull. When it had extended some six or eight feet, the Professor pushed down a lever and water began running into one of the tank compartments. In a few seconds, the compartment was full and he shut off the pump. Then, from the shelves which held emergency rations, he took a box of hard sea biscuits.

"Help yourselves," he said cheerily.

Joe looked into the tank. "But they're alive," he faltered.

"So are raw oysters," said Professor Bullfinch, "but I've seen you eat dozens of them, Joe. A scientist should never draw back from new experiences."

He calmly dipped up some of the plankton and put it on his cracker. "Delicious," he said after a bite. "Tastes like shrimp salad."

"Well, I guess after octopus and cactus nothing matters," said Danny and he took some of the plankton. "Hey! It really *is* good," he said.

Irene was already munching away, and Joe at last tasted a mouthful. Then he took another, and another, and went on eating until the Professor pointed out to him that they wanted to keep just a few of the tiny creatures as specimens.

The *Urchin* continued to descend. The plankton thinned away and vanished, and the water became clear again. Its blue tinge darkened.

"One thousand feet," Captain Beaversmith said. "We're below the level to which ordinary submarines can go. I think we'll stop here for a bit."

He pressed a button, and they heard a rattle as some of their shot ballast was released. The water had become colder, and the sides of the hull grew misty. He touched another button which started air circulating along the sides and quickly cleared away the mist. Dr. Grimes and Professor Bullfinch snapped the lights on in the cabin—very soft, shielded lights which allowed them to see what they were doing, but did not reflect on the walls and prevent their seeing outside.

Large jellyfish floated by, looking like parachutes with long tentacles trailing below them. An eel writhed into the searchlight beam and away again. Red and white shrimps kicked themselves around the lights like moths and then shot off as a huge dark shadow loomed up.

Irene gasped and clapped a hand over her mouth to keep from yelling. Danny exclaimed, "Jeepers!" The Professor beckoned to Dr. Grimes and called softly to the Captain, "Take a look at this, Beaversmith."

Writhing tentacles, longer than telephone poles, moved outside the ship. Then a vast white body with a tail shaped like a spearhead could be seen at the edge of the searchlights' glare. It was the size of a small house. A great, flat, round eye stared at the people in the ship.

"A s-s-sea dragon," Joe stammered.

"Not quite. It's a giant squid," Professor Bullfinch replied. "They have found pieces of such monsters on the surface and have estimated them to be about fifty feet in length. This one's closer to eighty."

"What'll we do?" Joe whimpered. "Will he g-g-grab us?"

"Oh, no, I hardly think so," said the Professor coolly. "I know that Hollywood movies and comic strips are always showing ships being attacked by giant squids, but the fact is they are probably extremely timid. Their greatest enemy is the killer whale, and this fellow may think we're something dangerous. In any case, he will know from the feel of our hull that the ship isn't alive."

As he spoke, a couple of tentacles touched the ship and they could feel the hull vibrate. Captain Beaversmith moved one of the light controls so a searchlight shone full on the giant beast. It moved back a little way.

"A splendid opportunity for a photograph," said the Professor. "Quick, Grimes, get some

They could feel the hull vibrate.

more plates. I'll start taking pictures with what we have in the cameras.''

The scientists clearly had no thought of possible danger, but were only concerned with their work. The Professor sprang to the camera controls, while Dr. Grimes darted off to get some additional film. Danny was excited by their courage and his own curiosity was aroused.

''I wonder what kind of sound a squid makes?'' he said to Irene.

Without hesitating any longer, he snatched up his tape recorder. ''Maybe I can drop the hydrophone outside through the collecting tank pump,'' he muttered.

He rushed to the tank. Then everything seemed to happen at once.

There were a number of very bright, sudden flashes like lightning in the water. These were the stroboscopic flashbulbs for the cameras going off. Startled, Danny turned his head. So did Dr. Grimes, who was running toward him with his arms full of film plates. They crashed into each other, and Dr. Grimes sat down abruptly. Danny's tape recorder fell to the floor.

Dr. Grimes turned crimson. ''Why don't you look where I'm going?'' he fumed.

''The squid has gone,'' said the Professor,

coming to help Dr. Grimes to his feet. "The lights must have frightened him. However, I'm sure I got a couple of good pictures."

Danny was examining his tape recorder. "Don't get excited, Dr. Grimes," he said soothingly. "The recorder wasn't hurt at all. Listen."

He turned it on. From the amplifier came a loud squawk.

Dr. Grimes jumped a foot in the air. The photographic plates flew from his arms and crashed to the deck.

"Oh, I'm sorry," Danny said. "That noise was the Common Spotfish—*Leiostomus xanthurus*."

Dr. Grimes's Adam's apple was bobbing up and down. He made a rapid ticking or clucking sound like that of the Common Sea Robin *(Prinotus carolinus)*. Then, finding his voice, he said, "Put—that—infernal—thing—away!"

"Wh-what?" Danny quavered.

"I said, 'Put that tape recorder away!'" Dr. Grimes roared. "And if you play it once more—just once more—on this voyage, I promise I will feed it—and you—to the fish!"

11
"Our Ship
Is Sinking!"

For a short time after Dr. Grimes's outburst, things were very quiet aboard the *Sea Urchin*. Captain Beaversmith began fussing with his controls; Professor Bullfinch busied himself about the cameras; and Dr. Grimes, as if somewhat ashamed of his temper, began working at the bench on some specimens. Danny looked about for a place to store his recorder.

"I can't put it on the floor," he whispered to Irene, "because somebody may trip over it and then I'll be blamed. And it looks as if every inch of space on the shelves is full of bottles or jars."

"How about underneath the collecting tank?" Irene said.

"Things are too busy around there," Danny frowned. Then his face brightened. *"There's the spot,"* he said.

Up forward, where Captain Beaversmith sat, the ship was crowded with instruments and gauges, but just above the pilot's seat there was an empty shelf. It was very narrow, but it would hold the tape recorder. Danny softly put his machine on this shelf—so softly that not even Captain Beaversmith noticed him—and lashed it down with a cord. About half of it stuck out over the shelf but at least it was out of the way.

Just as he got it stowed Captain Beaversmith said, "Professor! Dr. Grimes! Have a look at the sonar."

The two scientists hurried forward. The sonar was the device which bounced sound waves off the bottom and recorded their echoes. In this way, the various depths and the shape of the bottom could be observed on a screen. Dr. Grimes bent over this screen.

"A canyon," he muttered.

"No doubt of it," the Captain replied. "We didn't spot it on our other trips."

"We weren't exactly over this area," said the Professor. "My, my. It's nine thousand feet deep. Almost two miles. Perhaps we ought to explore it?"

"Not with the children aboard," said Dr. Grimes.

"No, of course not. Let's see if it's on the chart."

He went back to the chart table and pulled out a map showing the coastal waters. He and Dr. Grimes bent over it.

Captain Beaversmith pulled down a small handle on the control board, and then uttered an exclamation of annoyance. Danny, who was leaning on the back of his seat, said, "What's the matter, sir?"

"When those camera lights went off, something must have overloaded," the Captain said. "The tank pumps aren't responding. I'd better have a look-see."

He pulled up the cover on the control panel and began probing into the maze of wires inside. With a flashlight in one hand and an insulated screwdriver in the other, he began unfastening connections.

"Can I help?" Danny asked.

Captain Beaversmith, with his head buried in the control box, said, "Do you know anything about electricity?" At the same time, he put down his screwdriver and began fumbling among the loose wires that stuck up from the side of the box.

"Everything," said Danny boldly. "I learned

all about wiring when I was only a little kid. The Professor taught me. Here—is this the one you're looking for?''

He picked up one of the wires and thrust it into the Captain's hand. Captain Beaversmith took it automatically and connected it to something inside the control box.

There was a loud POP! Blue sparks sprang from the control board. Every light in the ship went out.

There was an instant of startled silence. Then everyone began talking or shouting at once:

''What's happened?''

"Put those lights on!"

"Captain Beaversmith—what are you doing?"

Danny heard a peculiar thump and then a groan. The flashlight rattled to the floor. He snatched it up. By its beam, he saw the pilot lying across the control panel.

The others made their way forward, guided by the light.

"What's the matter with Beaversmith?" Dr. Grimes barked.

"I think he was electrocuted," Danny gasped.

"Here, help me move him, Bullfinch," said Dr. Grimes. He and the Professor lifted the unconscious pilot and placed him on the deck.

Meanwhile, Danny looked into the control box. He found the wire he had given the Captain and disconnected it. Tracing the cables, he found the fuse box. One of the fuses had a burned filament. There were spare fuses in the box, and he replaced the burned one. At once the lights went on again.

"Good work, Dan," said Professor Bullfinch, blinking up at him.

But Danny wasn't listening. He was looking up at his tape recorder. It had been moved slightly. Then he glanced at the pilot's seat, directly under it. His heart sank.

"How on earth do you suppose it happened?" Dr. Grimes was saying. "I thought Beaversmith knew enough about electricity to keep from hurting himself."

"I don't think he was electrocuted after all," Danny said unhappily. "I think he was—er—bopped."

"Bopped?" said Dr. Grimes. "What are you talking about? Is that more fish language?"

"When the lights went out," said Dan, "he jumped up in alarm. I had put my recorder on the shelf above his head. He must have banged into it and knocked himself out."

"Aha! The tape recorder again!" cried Dr. Grimes.

"But I wasn't playing it, Dr. Grimes," said Danny. "I did just what you told me to do— I put it away. I didn't know he was going to jump up."

"And perhaps you can also tell us why the lights went out?" Dr. Grimes said, grinding his teeth. "I'll wager you had something to do with that, too."

"Now, then, Grimes, let's not jump to conclusions," the Professor put in.

Danny hung his head. "But he's right," he said in a very small voice. "I handed the Captain the wrong wire."

Dr. Grimes threw up his hands. The Professor shook his head and said, "Well, accidents can happen. At any rate, you got the lights back on, Dan. Now we'd better see to poor Beaversmith."

He examined the pilot, who had a bad gash on his scalp. "He's had a nasty crack," the Professor said. "I think he will be all right, though. We'd better bundle him up warmly and leave him alone. That's often the best first aid."

He and Dr. Grimes wrapped the Captain in a blanket and made him as comfortable as they could, considering the cramped space. To keep him from being moved about by any rocking or pitching the little ship might do when they returned to the surface, they lashed him snugly to the deck near the pilot's seat.

As they were tucking him in, Joe, who had been leaning on the chart table, said, "Professor Bullfinch, does it ever snow under water?"

"Snow under water?" the Professor repeated. "Your question sounds like English, Joe, but it doesn't make sense."

"No, I guess not. It must be my eyes then. Being under the sea does things to them." Joe sighed. "It looks to me," he went on mournfully, "as though it is snowing outside."

"Impossible," said Grimes, tightening the last knots around the Captain.

97

"I know," Joe went on. "Not only that—the snow is falling up."

The Professor stood up and stared out through the hull. Irene said, "Why—he's right! It *is* upside-down snow."

By the searchlights' glare they could see millions of white flakes streaming upward past the hull. Joe said, "You mean you can see it, too? Then there's nothing wrong with me. I feel better."

His mouth dropped open. "Wait a minute," he said. "I *don't* feel better. How can it be snowing? And upside down?"

"It can be explained easily," said the Professor, taking off his glasses and wiping them carefully. "There's no cause for alarm. Those flakes are another layer of plankton."

"Oh, I see." Joe blew out a breath of relief. "And they're swimming up past us, is that it?"

"On the contrary, they aren't moving at all," said the Professor. "Our ship is sinking."

12
On the Bottom

It took a few seconds for them to absorb this startling news. Then Joe let out a yelp.

"Abandon ship! S.O.S.! Women and children first!"

He stopped, looked puzzled, and said, *"I'm* a children. But we're under water already. How can we abandon ship?"

"Oh, what'll we do?" cried Irene. "Can't we stop it?"

"Keep cool," said the Professor. "Let's not lose our heads."

"We're all right, Professor," Danny said as bravely as he could. He took Irene's hand. "Aren't we, Irene?"

Irene gulped and nodded.

"I'm all right, too," Joe said. "All I have to do is stop my teeth from chattering so I can hear myself being brave."

"It's very simple to explain," the Professor said. "When the Captain fell, he must have hit the control which started the pumping of sea water into the ballast tanks. All we have to do is shut it off, empty the tanks, jettison our shot ballast and batteries, and rise to the surface."

"Very simple, indeed," said Dr. Grimes sourly. He had become very pale but kept his self-control with an effort. "Have you ever handled the controls of the ship, Bullfinch?"

"Well, no," the Professor admitted. "But it shouldn't be too difficult. Everything is marked clearly."

"I remember now," Danny put in, "while you and Dr. Grimes were looking at the charts, Captain Beaversmith said that the tank pumps weren't responding. I guess he meant they weren't working properly. He began to fix them, and that's when all the trouble started."

"Yes, and if it hadn't been for your meddling—" Dr. Grimes began fiercely.

"Now, now," said the Professor. "Quarreling won't get us back up, and it wastes time. Let's examine the control board."

He sat down in the pilot's seat and rested his chin on his hand.

"Whatever you do, you'd better hurry," said Dr. Grimes. "According to the depth gauge, we're already down to thirty-five hundred feet."

The Professor carefully studied all the controls. At last, turning around, he said, "I'm sorry. Everything is clearly marked: here are the buttons which control the propeller motors, the ballast release, the electromagnets, and all the rest of the equipment. But here—" He pointed to a slot on the panel. "Here, there must have been a lever which controlled the sea-water tanks. This small plate says 'Tank pumps.' But the lever itself is missing."

"Well, why not jettison the ballast and drop off the batteries?" said Dr. Grimes.

"We can drop the ballast, but that won't be enough to get us back to the surface," said the Professor. "And I hesitate to drop off our batteries until we absolutely have to, for that will deprive us of all our lights. If we sink to the bottom, I at least want to be able to look around."

"Very commendable," grumbled Dr. Grimes.

"It is possible that when the Captain fell," the Professor went on, "he may have been holding the lever, and it dropped to the deck. I suggest that we search for it."

For the next half hour they all but took the cabin to bits, looking for the missing lever. They searched every corner, lifted the cover of the control panel and looked under the wires, and inspected all the shelves, containers, and instruments.

Finally, the Professor straightened up with a sigh. "Well," he said, "it is probably staring us in the face, but it's so obvious that we can't see it. We shall have to give up for the time being."

"Then what are we to do?" Irene asked anxiously.

"Oh, we're not absolutely helpless," said the Professor. "We can move backward and forward, even if we can't move upward. We can, of course," he added drily, "continue to move downward, as well."

"I don't think so, Professor," said Danny slowly.

"Why not?" asked the Professor in surprise.

"Because I think we've landed." He pointed outside. "Aren't we on the bottom?"

The searchlights showed a gray, muddy plain stretching beneath them. They were floating some six feet above it. Danny sprang to the depth gauge.

"Nine thousand, four hundred feet," he said in a hushed tone.

The others were silent. Beyond the circle of their lights all was inky blackness. Above their heads the world of sunlight and air was nearly two miles away, and all about them stretched the vast ocean. In the utter quiet, Danny could hear the beating of his pulses. Their ship was no more than a tiny particle of light, a mere bubble at the bottom of the sea, and upon every square inch of it pressed a weight of more than two tons of water.

13
Feast and Fun

Professor Bullfinch was the first to speak. "We're not dead yet," he said.

Dr. Grimes was clutching the back of the pilot's seat with both hands. He looked pale and haggard. "It's only a matter of moments," he said. "We're doomed."

"Pull yourself together, Grimes," said the Professor sharply. "We're nothing of the sort. Sooner or later we'll figure out a way of getting back to the surface. Meanwhile, remember that we built this undersea laboratory in order to investigate the ocean bottom. Well, here we are on the bottom. We are scientists. Our duty is to learn all we can."

He looked round at them all, and his eyes

sparkled. "A scientist should fear nothing. Even death is only an experience to be studied. Let us do our work, and if by some chance we cannot escape, we can be certain that someday others will follow us, find us, and learn from our investigations."

"You're just making me gloomier," Joe said in a quavering voice. "But I see what you mean."

"I'm not afraid," Danny said. "Are you, Irene?"

"No, I'm not. I think the Professor's right."

"If you mean to imply that *I* was upset," said Dr. Grimes sternly, "you are wrong, Bull-finch. I merely felt—er—disturbed because of the young people. I am perfectly ready to continue with our investigations."

"Oh, I'm not sc-sc-scared either," Joe said. "I'm just empty."

"Exactly!" cried the Professor. "Joe has put his finger right on the trouble."

"I have?" said Joe in astonishment.

"Certainly. We're all hungry. What we need is a bite to eat and a little rest. Come on, Grimes, let's get out some rations."

They had plenty of emergency rations stacked away on a shelf: dried beef, cheese, chocolate bars, raisins, hard biscuits, and two five-gallon cans of fresh water. Clearing off the top of the laboratory workbench, they set out circles of filter paper for plates and spread their feast. Before they ate, the Professor examined Captain Beaversmith again; he was still unconscious but appeared to be breathing more easily. They all fell to on the provisions and ate heartily, and as the Professor had predicted, when their stomachs were full their spirits rose.

When they had cleared away the remains and were loosening their belts, the Professor said with a twinkle in his eyes, "Now, we ought to have some after-dinner music. What about a concert, Grimes?"

Both the scientists were enthusiastic amateur musicians; the Professor played the bull fiddle and Dr. Grimes the piccolo. Dr. Grimes, his long face looking a shade less severe, took his piccolo case down from a shelf, while the Professor got out his bull-fiddle bow and began rubbing it with rosin.

"Where's your bull fiddle?" Irene asked, looking about the cabin. There was no place in which to store such a large instrument.

"Oh," said the Professor airily, "it's in my pocket."

As the three young people gaped at him, he reached into a coat pocket and took out the strings to his bull fiddle, neatly coiled up and tied.

"But—but what are you going to fasten them to?" Danny said.

"Aha!" Professor Bullfinch winked. "Do you remember asking me about those hooks and eyes in the ceiling and floor?"

He went to them and, as he was fastening the fiddle strings to the eyes, said, "I will use the hull of the *Urchin* itself as my sounding board."

The hooks in the ceilings had turnbuckles on them so that they could be raised or lowered, and in this way he was able to tighten his strings and tune them to his liking. To make a bridge, he unbolted the pilot's seat from the floor and wedged its rounded back against the strings and its foot against the nearest wall. He was able to change the pitch of his strings by pinching them between his fingers. Then he announced that he was ready.

"What shall we play?" Dr. Grimes said, trying a run on his piccolo.

"Do you know the funeral march?" said Joe.

"Oh, shut up, Joe," said Danny. "Play something jolly, Professor."

The two men began a rollicking sailor's dance, the piccolo squeaking merrily against the zoom-zoom of the bull fiddle which made the whole cabin vibrate. Suddenly Dr. Grimes stopped playing.

"You're trying to drown me out," he said accusingly.

"I?" said the Professor in astonishment. "Why, my dear man, what gave you that idea? It's just that the bull fiddle has a richer, deeper tone than the piccolo."

"Richer tone? Absurd!" shouted Dr. Grimes. "The piccolo has a sweet, delicate tone. The bull fiddle makes a sound like—like one of Danny's fish noises. A croaker or a toadfish!"

"Nonsense," said the Professor. "But in any case, it is impossible for me to play any softer."

"Ha! Then I will play louder," said Dr. Grimes. He glared about. "Danny! Where's that tape recording machine?"

Danny raised his eyebrows. "But Dr. Grimes—you told me not to touch it."

"Quite right. But I'm going to touch it, not you. Get it for me, please."

Danny untied the lashings and took down the case.

"If I am correct," said Dr. Grimes, "it is possible to play through the amplifier of one of these machines directly, as if through a public-speaking apparatus."

He opened the case, hooked up the microphone, snapped the switch and began to play. No sound emerged at all.

"Something's wrong with your machine," he growled, snapping the switch on and off.

"I—uh—I think you're recording instead of playing through the amplifier," said the Professor. "I suggest you let Danny fix it for you."

Dr. Grimes grumbled, but he allowed Danny to make the necessary adjustments. Then he played into the microphone once more. This time, the notes of the piccolo came out of the amplifier with a blast like a policeman's whistle.

"Fine!" said he with a grim smile. "Now that we're even, Bullfinch, let's try our duet again."

They began to play once more, and the three young people held their hands over their ears. But Dr. Grimes seemed very satisfied, and Professor Bullfinch, although he kept wincing and ducking his head as the shrill notes flew about him, played on resignedly out of pure friendship. At last the terrible concert was over.

The Professor put his bow and fiddle strings away, and Dr. Grimes packed up his piccolo. Danny changed the adjustment on his tape re-

Professor Bullfinch played on out of friendship.

corder and put it back on the shelf with a wistful sigh.

Then Professor Bullfinch said, "Now, friends, we've had our feast and our fun, and I think it's time to go to work."

"Very well," said Dr. Grimes, forgetting that he was supposed to be the leader of the expedition. "What do you suggest?"

"We can still move the ship horizontally," said the Professor, putting his empty pipe in his mouth (for because of the cramped space and lack of ventilation, he did not smoke in the ship). "Let us permit one of the young people to steer the *Urchin*. The others can control the lights and the collecting devices. You and I, Grimes, will begin taking core samples from the bottom."

"Hmm." Dr. Grimes gazed at the three young people. "Bullfinch, you have demonstrated an astonishing lack of practical good sense in the past, but this suggestion 'takes the cake,' as the saying goes. Do you seriously mean to propose that one of these children should hold the wheel?"

The Professor chuckled. "I knew you'd see things my way," he said. "You're right! After all, the ship moves very slowly, and starting and stopping it is a simple matter of pressing a button. Steering it is equally simple. All we need do is choose the most responsible and levelheaded of the young people—''

Danny smiled bashfully, kicking at the deck with one toe. ''Gee, thanks, Professor,'' he began.

''—Irene, for instance,'' the Professor finished firmly.

14
The Shark

The *Urchin* moved slowly forward through the dark strange world of the sea bottom. Irene sat in the pilot's seat, peering forward through the clear plastic of the bows. The controls were essentially very simple: a small wheel turned the rudder to port and starboard, a set of buttons sent the ship forward, held it still, or put it in reverse. She gripped the wheel tightly, trying to relax and breathe normally; she felt very proud and a little frightened to have the steering of the whole vessel in her charge. "Now," she said to herself, "I know what the captain of a ship really feels like."

Behind her, in the after end of the cabin, Dan stood ready at the mechanical arms, while

Joe lounged near him at the collecting tank. In the middle of the ship the two scientists were busy preparing their coring apparatus.

This consisted of a metal tube some ten feet long and six inches in diameter. One end was sharpened. The tube was put upright into a cylindrical air chamber that ran from the conning tower hatch down through the floor, with an air lock at the bottom. The upper end of the tube was hooked to a wire cable which was wound around a drum at the top of the air chamber.

When they had made all their preparations, Professor Bullfinch called, "Irene, stop the ship."

"Aye aye, sir," Irene said a bit nervously. She tapped the button which stopped the motors. The ship slowed, drifted for a moment or two, and then came to a standstill.

The Professor pulled a lever. There was a *whoosh* as the tube was shot out of the air chamber. It plunged deep into the soft sea bottom where it filled up with mud, like a soda straw jabbed into ice cream. They saw a cloud of silt rise from the bottom. Dr. Grimes pulled another lever and the drum turned, winding up the cable and drawing the tube back into the air chamber. The water was forced out through the lock, and then the tube could be removed from the chamber. The ooze with which the chamber was filled—it was called a "core sample"—was taken out and the scientists began their study of it.

After three or four times, the core sampling lost its novelty for the young people, and they began to pay more attention to the water around them. The lights of the ship made a large circle on the yellowish-gray mud below, and they could see that the sea floor was not smooth but covered with ripples. Among these ripples lay what appeared to be pebbles, although it was hard to say how pebbles came to be scattered over the bottom of the ocean.

"Perhaps they're some kind of animal," Danny suggested to the others. "Shellfish, maybe."

"Wonder if they're good to eat," said Joe.

"We can ask the Professor when he's done with his work. Look, there are some of those hatchetfish they had in the collecting tank."

Danny pointed. Alongside the hull of the *Urchin* swam a dozen tiny, glittering fish, like jewels floating in the murky water. Their round eyes and gaping mouths made it seem they were wondering what kind of monster the ship was.

"I've got their sounds on tape," Danny said. "Remember? *Chirp, chirp, chirp!*" He put his mouth close to the side of the hull. "Hey, fish!" he called. *"Cheep, cheep!"*

The hatchetfish flicked their tails, turning so that the lights along their bellies flashed. They shot away into the darkness.

"You probably said something insulting in fish talk," said Joe. "Like, 'Get the hook.' "

"Whatever I said, I'll bet they couldn't hear me through three inches of plastic," Danny laughed. "But isn't it fun being able to see these things just as if we lived down here? It's better than an aquarium."

"Better?" said Joe glumly. "It's the same thing as an aquarium. Only we're the ones in the tank—an air tank instead of a tank of water. Wonder if the fish think somebody put us down here for them to study?"

"I wonder," Irene said thoughtfully, "if there could be any people living on the ocean floor?"

"Well, sure there are," said Joe. "You, me, the Professor, Dr. Grimes—I don't know whether we can count Danny as people—"

"Oh!" Irene interrupted. "What a beautiful fish!"

The two boys went up to the pilot's seat. Through the clear plastic bows they could see, at the edge of the circle of light, a large, flat, pearly creature. It had a tiny mouth and eyes that were no more than pinpoints. Its smooth body, which seemed to have no scales, glowed like a moon.

Irene touched a control button and sent the ship forward a little way so that she could see the fish better.

"Here, what are you up to?" cried Dr. Grimes. "Hold steady."

"Sorry." Irene stopped the ship again. The pearly fish turned and swam back to the left, parallel with the ship but just outside the light. Then Irene gasped, "Oh! Look!"

A monstrous blue-green shape, paler below than above, glided into view on the right. It had a flat snout shaped like a shovel, and round milky-white eyes, and when it turned they could see the cruel teeth in its down-curved mouth.

"A shark," whispered Danny. "What a whopper! He's almost as big as the ship."

"Oh, Danny," said Irene. "Do something! He's going to attack that lovely little fish."

"Little fish?" Joe repeated. "Oh, man! Girls sure do get their sizes mixed up. That little fish is the same size as the shark."

"But his mouth is smaller," Irene said, wringing her hands. "Danny, can't you do something?"

The pearly creature was at the stern of the

Urchin by now, and the shark slid toward it along the other side. There was something tigerish about the way the shark moved that made the young people shiver. Danny rushed to the stern and thrust his arms into the metal sleeves that controlled the jointed arms and claws outside the hull.

As the shark came even with the stern of the ship and began to turn on its side, Danny raised one of the arms. He grabbed for the shark's sharp tail and tried to pinch it. The metal claws rasped against the rough hide of the fish, which was too tough for them.

But the shark's attention was attracted, away from the pearly creature and to the *Urchin*. He turned like lightning and snapped his great jaws against the side of the ship. The plastic was too strong for him to penetrate, but the ship rocked under the blow.

Both Professor Bullfinch and Dr. Grimes had been too busy to notice what was happening. But now, they were almost knocked off their feet. They tried to steady themselves, shouting questions and commands at once.

Danny kept his balance and punched at the shark with the right-hand claw. He hit the creature hard and hurt it. The monster doubled around. Its jaws clashed on the metal arm and made two large dents in it. Then it turned on its side and swam straight for the *Urchin*. Once more the wicked teeth scraped the smooth plastic, and the people inside were jolted about helplessly by the violence of the attack.

"Help! What'll we do?" yelled Joe. He was almost thrown to the deck by another blow against the ship. He grabbed for something to cling to and his hand closed about the lever that worked the suction pump. The pump started.

"That's it!" Danny cried. "We'll trap him so he can't move."

He staggered to the collecting tank, which was rapidly filling with water. He seized the wheel which controlled the flexible intake pipe. He turned it toward the shark just as the beast made another rush at the ship.

The shark's snout slammed into the suction intake and stuck there tightly.

15
"It's Gold!"

The ship rolled and pitched as if caught in a storm. Struggling to get free, the shark lashed its tail and jerked its huge body from side to side, but its snout was jammed in the intake valve, and the suction of the powerful pump motor held it firmly. The people in the ship were banged about unmercifully. They hung on to whatever they could to keep from being bruised.

"Can't we do something?" Joe groaned. "I'm beginning to feel like a tossed salad."

The Professor was clutching the side of the laboratory bench. He said, "I expected to do a certain amount of collecting of specimens, but it looks as though this specimen is trying

to collect us. How on earth did you get us into this, Dan?"

"I'm sure it was easy for a boy with his talents," said Dr. Grimes. He was underneath one of the shelves with his feet braced against the wall. "I didn't expect to end my career inside a shark."

"As a matter of fact," said Professor Bullfinch, "I believe this is a member of the *Squalidae,* one of the dogfish family. Very interesting. As you know, the sharks and dogfish are living fossils, survivals from the Devonian Age, millions of years ago. Instead of scales they have plates of shagreen on their bodies, and their teeth are simply enlarged sections of this rough skin—"

124

"You are an idiot, Bullfinch!" shouted Dr. Grimes. "It's not a dogfish but a Port Jackson shark. Look at the dorsal fins—"

"Tut, tut," said the Professor, "I really believe—"

"Can I say something?" shouted Irene over the noise.

"Dear me, do you think it's a Port Jackson shark, too?" said the Professor mildly.

"I was just going to say that Danny ought to just shut off the suction pump," Irene said.

Almost before the words were out of her mouth, Danny was at the lever. Water was splashing over the sides of the tank and he was soaked, but he grabbed the lever and pushed it. The pump stopped. But the shark was by now wedged so tightly into the intake that this made very little difference.

"No good," Danny gasped, holding the tank with one hand and trying to wipe the water out of his eyes with the other.

"One reverse after another," cried Dr. Grimes angrily. "First Beaversmith's accident, and then—"

But Danny interrupted him. "Reverse? That's it!"

He seized the lever and pulled it over as far as it would go into the "Reverse" position.

The motor whined, and suddenly all the

125

water in the collecting tank vanished into the hose. At the same time, Joe cried, "He's out!"

When the motor was reversed, a strong current of water and air shot out through the hose. They saw the shark literally blown backward in the water, away from the ship. He hung still for a moment as if dazed by his experience, then flapped his tail frantically and was out of sight before they could blink.

"That'll teach him not to play with strangers," said Joe. "Oh, my back. I'll never be the same again."

"Neither will that dogfish," said Danny, rubbing a bruise on his arm.

"Port Jackson shark, you mean," said Dr. Grimes, crawling from under the shelf. He went to the air chamber. He threw the switch to pull the core sampling tube up from the mud. There was a rattling sound. He opened the chamber.

"More trouble!" he said. "This is really too much."

"What's the matter?" asked the Professor.

"Look for yourself. During all that banging about, the cable was broken. We've lost the core sampler."

He sat down with his head in his hands and groaned. The Professor patted his shoulder. "Be calm, Grimes," he said. "After all, we did take a number of samples. And we can have another tube sent to us—when we get back to the surface.''

"When?" moaned Dr. Grimes. *"When* we get back? Do you seriously think we'll ever escape?''

"Keep your spirits up,'' said the Professor. "How is our captain?'' he added, turning to Irene. "Are you all right? We can't afford to have another pilot put out of action.''

"I'm all right,'' Irene said. "Just a little bumped. But come up forward, Professor. There's something very odd ahead.''

"Another shark—or Port Dogson jackfish— or whatever I mean?'' said Joe.

Irene sent the ship forward a little way. The lights shone on a high wall of mud, which towered up before them.

"Ah, that's one side of the canyon into which we've dropped,'' said the Professor.

"Yes. And do you see that shiny thing near the bottom?'' said Irene.

Projecting from the mud was what looked like part of a wheel. But in the lights it gleamed brightly, like a stray piece of sunshine.

They had all gathered behind the pilot's seat by now, and suddenly Joe said, "I know what it is.''

They all stared at him. Slowly and dramatically he drew from his pocket a folded piece of parchment.

"The Aztec treasure?" Danny burst out. "Gosh! I wonder—"

"For all we know," said Joe, "it's right on the spot marked with a cross. Why couldn't it be?"

"Aztec treasure?" Dr. Grimes said. "What sort of rubbish is this?"

"Better explain, Joe," said the Professor. "I'm afraid I don't understand."

Quickly, Joe told the story of the Sun Image, as Ramon had narrated it. When he was finished, the Professor went close to the side of the hull and peered out at the golden thing.

"Thorough nonsense," barked Dr. Grimes. "It is probably a piece of brasswork from some ship."

"I don't think so, Grimes," said the Professor. "Brass would have corroded in the water. Copper would have turned green. This is still shiny in spite of the mud and shellfish all over it. It is certainly very interesting. . . ."

"Hum," said Danny in a soft voice and with a sly, sideways look at the Professor. "I wonder what sort of shellfish those are."

"Yes. A good point," said the Professor, rubbing his chin.

"It wouldn't be too hard to get it into the ship," Irene said, as if to herself.

"You're right. I think we ought to try," said the Professor. "Grimes, what do you say?"

Dr. Grimes frowned. "I doubt that it is an Aztec treasure, or any other kind of treasure," he said. "But it is certainly an odd shape and color. Perhaps we ought to investigate it."

He and the Professor went to the after part of the cabin, while Irene carefully turned the ship until its stern was directly over the shining object. Dr. Grimes put his arms into the hanging sleeves, while the Professor bent over the air lock on the floor. This was a round hatchway with two covers and a good-sized space between them. Pressing a lever, the Professor opened the outer cover. Then Dr. Grimes maneuvered the claws and tried to pick up the golden thing. He grunted and muttered to himself, for it was deeply buried, but at last he pulled it free and set it inside the lock. The Professor closed the outer cover. The water was automatically pumped out of the lock. They opened the inner cover and bent over their catch.

It took both men to pull it up into the cabin, for it was very heavy, and in addition, it was encrusted with mud and tiny shells. It was

round and thick and carved with Aztec figures of men and beasts, and even Dr. Grimes was forced to admit that it was clearly something old and valuable.

The Professor let out a long breath. "No doubt of it," he said. "It's gold. And it is definitely ancient Aztec."

"An image of the sun, I would say," said Dr. Grimes. "And see here, Bullfinch, on the other side is a carving of Quetzalcoatl, the Feathered Serpent."

"I knew it," said Joe. "This thing must be worth a fortune."

"Not in money, Joe," the Professor said gravely. "If we are right, it is priceless. It's a historical treasure, and no one can say what it is worth."

"What—" Danny began and then stopped short. The others froze, as well. In the cabin behind them sounded a dismal, hollow groan.

16
Trapped!

It was Captain Beaversmith. He was awake and trying to rise, but the lashings, which had kept him from being thrown about during the shark's attack, held him fast. His tanned face was very pale, but otherwise he seemed quite normal.

"Where are we?" he mumbled. "What's happened?"

Irene got to him first. "Dear Captain Beaversmith," she said, dropping to her knees. "Do you feel better?"

"That's a difficult question," he said with a wan smile. "Better than what? My head seems to have come loose."

"Please lie down and rest," said Irene, pulling the edge of the blanket up over him again.

"Yes, you've had a rough time of it," said the Professor. "Better take it easy."

Danny got out another blanket, rolled it up, and tucked it under the Captain's head, while Dr. Grimes unfastened the lashings and made him more comfortable. Captain Beaversmith sank back with a sigh.

"I can't seem to recall what happened," he said. "There was a short circuit, wasn't there? I jumped up—and that's all I remember."

"You hit your head on my tape recorder," Danny explained. "It was on the shelf above your seat."

"Tapped by a tape," murmured the Captain. He closed his eyes wearily. "I see. And where are we now?"

"I'm afraid you must prepare yourself for a shock," said the Professor. "We are on the sea bottom."

The Captain blinked. "On the bottom? The blow must have done something to my eyes. I can't see a thing outside the hull."

"Dear me," said Professor Bullfinch. "We have all the searchlights on."

"Are you sure, Professor?" Danny put in, in a strained voice.

"Yes, of course. Why?"

"Because the blow on the Captain's head must have done something to *my* eyes, too. I can't see anything out there either."

It was true. Outside the hull was a solid wall

of dark yellow, as if they had been rolled up in wrapping paper. They stared and rubbed their eyes, and Captain Beaversmith said, "In my experience, that can only mean one thing. Mud."

"Mud?" Dr. Grimes repeated in surprise.

"Help me up, old chap," said the Captain.

The Professor and Dr. Grimes took his arms and helped him get to his feet. He shook his head to clear it.

"I'm still a bit groggy," he said, "but I can manage. Now, then. We were above an undersea canyon just before I took my little nap. Did you decide to descend into it?"

"Not exactly," said the Professor. "We didn't decide. We just descended."

"Ah, I remember now. The sea-water tank pumps weren't working properly. But didn't you even try to pull the lever?"

"We couldn't," the Professor said. "It was gone. We looked everywhere for it, but couldn't find it."

Captain Beaversmith took his chin in his hand. "That's odd," he said. "I'm almost sure I was holding it. . . . Well, first things first. So you sank into the canyon, is that it?"

"Yes. In fact, we pulled the sun image out of one wall of the canyon," the Professor replied.

"Sun image? What on earth do you mean?"

"It's an ancient Aztec relic. There it is, on the deck."

The Captain inspected it. "Handsome bit of jewelry," he said. "Pretty valuable, I shouldn't wonder. Well, that explains it."

He returned to the pilot's seat and sat down with a sigh. "When you pulled that golden pie dish out of the canyon wall," he went on, "you started the soft mud falling. It turned into an undersea avalanche, an avalanche of sand and mud. We are surrounded by a cloud of the stuff held suspended in the water." He looked pensively through the nose of the ship. "Looks like a real London pea-soup fog, it does. Makes me feel quite homesick."

"It's the saltiest pea soup I ever saw," Danny said.

"Stop it," begged Joe.

"Why? Am I scaring you?"

"No, you're making me hungry."

Dr. Grimes interrupted. "What do you suggest, Captain?"

"To begin with, can we move at all?"

"The propellers are still working," said the Professor.

"Good. Then let's try backing out of this mud cloud, if we can. We'll be able to work better in clear water." Captain Beaversmith took the controls and slowly sent the ship backward.

They could see that they were moving because the particles of sand all around them moved past the hull. They traveled for fifteen or twenty minutes with no sign of the cloud thinning, and suddenly the ship stopped with a bump. Fortunately, they were going very slowly.

"What now?" Dr. Grimes asked.

"I believe we've just touched the opposite wall of the canyon." The Captain shut off the motors. "Well, since we can't get free of the mud cloud, let's have a look at the pump control."

He opened the cover and bent over the wiring with a screwdriver and pliers. He worked in silence as they watched anxiously, and finally he raised his head.

"Done!" he said. "I believe the pumps will work now. The question is, where's the lever?"

He leaned back in the seat with a worried look and thrust his hands into his pockets. Then, slowly, his face changed: first, he scowled at the ceiling, then he began to laugh.

"Grimes!" the Professor whispered. "It's the blow on his head. He's getting hysterical."

"I'll grab one arm, and you grab the other," said Grimes.

But before they could move, Captain Beaversmith slowly took his hands out of his pockets. In his right hand was the missing lever.

"There's one place you didn't search," he said. "I remember, now. To get the cover off the control board, it is necessary to unscrew the lever. For safekeeping, I put it in my pocket. I'm sorry, I'm afraid it was a little *too* safely kept."

They all sighed with relief, and Dr. Grimes almost smiled. Quickly, the Captain replaced the lever.

"Right!" he said. "Now, I'm going to drop the ballast and blow the sea-water tanks. Got torches handy?"

The Professor took out several large battery-powered lanterns and lighted them.

"Jolly good," said the Captain. "Going up, gents."

He pressed several buttons and threw over the lever. The lights went out as the batteries which supplied them were disconnected, and they heard a thunderous rumble which meant the heavy battery cases were dropping from the deck above. The shot ballast went rattling out of its silo, and they could hear the hissing of the pumps as the water in the outer ballast tanks was forced out. The Professor handed a lantern to Dr. Grimes and placed another on the control board next to the Captain."

"Are we going up?" Joe whispered to Danny. "I can never feel any movement."

"That's because there's no vibration, I guess," Danny answered.

Just as he finished speaking, the ship jarred under their feet. It was like being in an elevator which had stopped short.

Captain Beaversmith glanced up. "Shine one of those flashlights through the side," he snapped. "See if the mud particles are moving."

Dr. Grimes hastened to do as he asked. "Nothing appears to be moving," he said.

The Captain glanced at a couple of dials. "The vertical speed indicator isn't registering," he said. "And the depth gauge shows that we're still down around nine thousand feet."

"You mean, something's holding us down?" said Dr. Grimes. "But what? We've dropped all our ballast. Why don't we ascend?"

"Maybe it's a—a giant squid," quavered Joe.

Captain Beaversmith shook his head. "Not likely," he said. "One can only surmise, of course, but I suspect that we have gone in under an overhanging ledge, or perhaps into a cave of some sort. We are bumping against the top of it."

"Well, but—but—can't we move at all?" said Irene.

"We can still move forward and backward," said the Captain. "The propeller batteries are inside the ship."

"Then let's move!" said Dr. Grimes. "What are you waiting for? Let's get out of here."

"A good point," said the Captain quietly. "The only problem is that we don't know where we are. So it's a bit difficult to know how to get out. For all we know, the mouth of the cave—if it is a cave—may have been covered up by the avalanche."

Dr. Grimes sank slowly to a seat. "Then we're trapped!"

"I'll admit, it is rather sticky," said the Captain. "Our best chance is to wait for the cloud of mud to settle. Then, perhaps by using our flashlights we can see through the hull and find our way out."

"Hmmmm," said the Professor. "And suppose it takes hours—or days—for the mud to settle."

"That," said the Captain, "might be decidedly awkward."

17
Water, Water, Everywhere. . . .

For a few moments which seemed as long as a year, the explorers said nothing. A weight of depression, even greater than they had felt earlier, settled on them. It was hard, after being so close to freedom, to have it snatched away again.

Dr. Grimes said in a dull voice, "Our air won't last forever. And what about food?"

"Air isn't the major problem with the purification system we have," said the Captain. "It's fresh water I'm worrying about. We haven't very much—less than ten gallons among the six of us."

"Seems funny," Danny said, trying hard to smile, "to think of dying of thirst under water."

"We could change the old poem," said the

Captain. " 'Into the jaws of death rode the six of us. Water to right of us, water to left of us. . . .' And so on."

"Don't tell me who wrote it," Joe said dolefully. "I don't like it. It's too realistic."

Danny turned to the Professor. "What do you say, Professor Bullfinch?"

"I don't think we ought to waste valuable breath or time on worry," the Professor answered with his usual cheeriness. "I suggest that we relax. Keep as quiet as possible so we don't waste energy. Something will turn up."

He took one of the lanterns and went back to the middle of the ship. He bent over the Sun Image and began scraping off some of the mud and shellfish which covered it.

"What are you doing?" Danny said.

"Well, I thought while I was waiting, I might as well do a little analyzing of this material from the floor of the sea," said the Professor. He carried his specimens to the laboratory bench, put the lantern nearby, and set to work.

"Do as you like, Bullfinch," said Dr. Grimes in a hollow tone. "I am going to make my last will and testament."

And he took out a piece of paper and a fountain pen and began writing.

Captain Beaversmith got up and went to his blanket. "For my part," he said, "I'm going to follow the Professor's suggestion. I'm still a bit fuzzy from that rap on the skull. I'm going to get some rest. You youngsters take my torch and shine it through the side from time to time. As soon as the water begins to clear, call me."

The three young people huddled down together on the floor near the control board. Dan held the lantern pressed against the plastic wall and from time to time snapped it on. Each time, the same yellow-gray curtain met his gaze.

"What do you think, Dan?" Irene said softly. "Will we ever get back?"

"I don't know," said Danny. "But I do know that I'm going to try to act like a real scientist—like the Professor. He isn't afraid of anything, and neither am I . . . I guess."

But in spite of his words, he swallowed hard.

Irene put her head on her knees. "You're right. I'm going to try to be the same. But it—it isn't easy."

Joe said, "This is real trouble. Worse than I can remember. You know how I know it? Because I don't feel hungry any more—just scared."

"You predicted it, Joe," Danny said, trying to joke. "Remember, long ago, when the Professor first said they might make an undersea ship out of the plastic? You said you knew there was trouble waiting for us at the bottom of the sea.''

"Yeah,'' said Joe. "Somebody must have been listening to me and didn't want me to be disappointed. Well, okay. I'm not.''

They fell silent, and the minutes ticked by. Joe and Irene dozed off to sleep in spite of their worry, for it had been a long day, full of excitement and tension. Danny remained wide awake. His mind was too full of guilt to let him rest.

"It's all my fault,'' he said to himself. "If only I hadn't thought so much of my tape recorder, and more about everybody's welfare. Instead of worrying about whether the recorder was broken, I should have thought of poor Dr. Grimes's film. If only I hadn't put the machine on that shelf! If only I hadn't meddled with those wires!''

He sighed. "Oh, gee. Why don't I have the sense not to jump into things without thinking them out first?''

He looked down at Irene and Joe, who were lying on either side of him. Then he sighed again and got up, carefully so as not to disturb them. He went to the bench where the Professor was examining something in a test tube.

"Professor Bullfinch," Danny said in a low voice.

"Yes, my boy?"

"I—I really feel awful."

The Professor raised his eyebrows. "Stomachache?"

"No, I don't mean that kind of awful. I mean, I feel that this mess is all my fault. We wouldn't be stuck down here if it weren't for me."

"Hmm. I see. You mean that you persuaded us to go on this expedition, is that it?"

"Well, no, of course not."

The Professor put his hands on Danny's shoulders. "My dear boy," he said, "I'll admit you have a habit of acting somewhat hastily. But we all wanted to come, and when we did we took the risk of accidents happening. I said that I would be personally responsible for your coming along. It was the Captain who jumped up in alarm, instead of sitting calmly in his seat as he should have done. It was I who said we should pull out the Sun Image, and Dr. Grimes who pulled it out, thus causing the avalanche."

Danny nodded. "Yes, you're right. But still, I promise I'm not going to act without thinking, from now on. And," he added firmly, "I promise I won't touch my tape recorder any more, either."

"Very well," said the Professor.

Danny went back to his place feeling a little better and knelt down. He took up the flashlight and shone it through the hull.

The water was clearing. There was still a great deal of mud floating in it, but the beam of his light now shot out for several feet in a misty glow. And twinkling like a tiny star just outside that beam was a hatchetfish.

Danny pressed his face against the plastic. *"Chirp!"* he whispered. *"Chirp, cheep!"*

As if it could hear him, the little fish swam closer to the hull. It darted through the beam of the light and away again. And Danny could see it shimmering in the darkness beyond for a second or two before it vanished.

"If only I could really talk fish language," he thought. "I could ask the hatchetfish to tell us the way out of here. . . ."

He paused and stared into space. Then he sprang to his feet. He ran to the Professor and grabbed his arm.

"Listen!" he shouted. "I know how to do it. I know how to get us out of here! Please let me take back my word—*Please!"*

The Professor's jaw dropped. "What? What word? What are you talking about?"

"My promise," Danny gasped. "Please let me play my tape recorder!"

18
Talking to the Fish

"The boy's gone crazy," said Dr. Grimes, putting down his pen.

"Just a minute." Professor Bullfinch raised his hand. "Now, Danny, get hold of yourself. You're not joking, are you?"

"No, *sir,*" Danny said as earnestly as he could. "I mean it. Can I play the recorder?"

Captain Beaversmith, who had been awakened by the first shout, got up from the floor rubbing his eyes. "Look here, old son," he said, "I may be dreadfully stupid, but I don't see how a tape recorder is going to get us out of here, unless you plan to broadcast a cry for help on it."

"I do," said Danny.

Irene and Joe had jumped up, too, and Joe said sarcastically, "Who are you going to broadcast to—the fish?"

"Yes," said Danny.

"You see," Dr. Grimes said sorrowfully, "he's raving mad. Now, then, Dan, just quiet down. Here, Bullfinch—let's wrap him in a blanket since we haven't got a strait jacket."

"Wait a minute," Danny protested, getting the lab bench between himself and the others. "Let me explain, will you? Now look—I've got a recording of the sounds the hatchetfish make. If I play it, by pressing the amplifier against the side of the hull and using the ship itself as a sounding board, maybe it will attract lots of hatchetfish to us."

The Professor blinked. And Captain Beaversmith said with a chuckle, "By George, the boy's got something. And you mean, they'd light up the water so we could see our way clear to leave?"

"I don't think they'd give that much light," Danny said. "But I just saw one out there— the water is clearing—and then he swam off and disappeared. Well, if they come, they've got to come from somewhere, don't they? So when they leave, all we have to do is follow them, and maybe they'll lead us out of this cave."

The Captain snapped his fingers. "I think it would work," he said.

"It's certainly worth trying," said the Professor. "What do you say, Grimes?"

"I think—" Dr. Grimes looked down at the paper on which he had been writing his will. Then he looked at Danny and then at the Professor. With one quick movement, he tore the paper in half and tossed it to the deck. "Let's do it!" he said.

Danny didn't wait to be told twice. He ran and got his tape recorder down from the shelf. Quickly, he rewound the tape to where the hatchetfish recording began. Pressing the amplifier against the side of the hull as tightly as he could, he started the machine.

The others waited breathlessly. Over and over again, Danny played his machine. Suddenly Irene cried, "There's one!"

"There's another," said Joe.

In the darkness, little pink torches flickered. More and more hatchetfish appeared: five, ten, then dozens. They clustered about the hull and their large eyes and mouths made them look like a crowd of curious goblins. The water shone from their pale lights.

"It works!" croaked Dr. Grimes.

Joe and Irene were jigging with excitement. Professor Bullfinch, cleaning his glasses absent-mindedly on a piece of muddy filter paper, said, "Wonderful! But how are you going to get them to leave?"

"I've thought of that, too," Danny said. "Watch."

He started the recorder again. And suddenly, in formation like a fleet of ships, the hatchetfish streamed away and in a few seconds were gone.

"Dear me," said the Professor. "How did you do that?"

"Easy," said Danny, unable to keep a note of pride out of his voice. "The next recording on the tape is the sound of viperfish. You told me the viperfish is the enemy of the hatchetfish, remember? I just played that sound, and the hatchetfish took off."

Captain Beaversmith eased himself into the pilot's seat. He put his hands on the controls. "All ready," he said. "Call 'em back, Dan. And tip me off when you start the viperfish noises so I can follow when they swim away."

Once again, Danny played the recording of the hatchetfish. Back came the tiny lanterns in the water. "Okay," he called to the Captain and started the machine again. This time, as the little fleet darted away, Captain Beaversmith moved the *Urchin* after them. He was

Danny played the recording of the hatchetfish.

able to follow their glow for quite a distance before losing them.

"Once again," he said.

Danny repeated the operation, and they followed the hatchetfish still further. And all at once, the Professor, who had been leaning over the Captain's shoulder, pointed to the dials on the control panel.

"The vertical speed indicator is moving," he said.

Sure enough, the needle was creeping up from zero.

"We must be out of the cave. We're rising," said the Captain in a tense voice. "Look at the depth gauge."

It registered a depth of eighty-five hundred feet.

Still, they could not quite believe it. They all stood quietly, waiting and watching. Steadily the needles of the two dials moved. They were going faster now, and the Captain mumbled, "Seven thousand . . . six thousand eight hundred . . . six thousand five hundred. . . ."

Danny gazed up through the ceiling. A bluish light filled the water above them. "Sky color!" he exclaimed.

Irene threw her arms about him and kissed him. Then she grinned and said, "Why, Danny

Dunn! The water's almost light enough for me to see you blush.''

Half an hour later, the *Urchin* bobbed up above the surface and brilliant sunlight filled the cabin.

Joe took a deep breath. "The Mexicans can keep the sun image," he sighed. "Real sunshine's the only gold I want."

19
Treasures
of the Sea

The restaurant of the Hotel Grande had never
seen such festivities as there were that night.
Around a long table decorated with flowers sat
the happy six; the three young people on one
side, and the three adults on the other, toasting
each other in Mexican lemon soda and stuffing
themselves with a delicious dish called *molé*—
it was made of turkey with a sauce of almonds,
peppers, spices and nuts, which the beaming
hotel cook had made in their honor. When they
could hold no more, they pushed their chairs
back and the waiter put steaming cups of thick
hot chocolate before them.

"Whew!" said Danny. "It was worth going through that adventure for a meal like this."

"You mean the appetizer we just had?" said Joe innocently. "Gosh, I was just wondering when we were going to start eating."

Professor Bullfinch pushed his glasses up on his forehead and stared at Joe. He said to Dr. Grimes, "You know, it would be fascinating to take this boy to pieces for the sake of science. How can he stuff so much into himself and remain so thin?"

"A good thing we're none of us very fat," said Captain Beaversmith. "We would have had to throw someone overboard. There isn't much room in the *Urchin*, and any extra weight might have held us down. 'Never weather-beaten sail more willing bent to shore. . . .' Thomas Campion."

Joe cleared his throat. "Speaking of poetry," he said modestly, "I—um—I have written a small poem for this occasion. I don't suppose anybody would like to hear it. . . ."

"I don't know if I can bear poetry on top of that big dinner," said Danny.

"—so I will recite it anyway," Joe went on.

"Go ahead, Joe," said Dr. Grimes. "After the ocean floor, nothing can frighten us."

Joe stood up, took out a sheet of paper, and after bowing to the company, began to read:

"I like rattlesnake steak,
And pine-needle pudding and rose-petal cake,
But if someone should brew a kinkajou stew
Flavored with library paste—
I wonder how it would taste?

I like grasshopper tips,
And octopus omelet and pollywog pips,
But if someone should stuff some moths in a muff
And then proceed to dry them and fry them—
I wonder if I'd dare to try them?

I like all types of grass,
And whale blubber suet and snipes under glass,
But if someone should roast a goblin or ghost
And serve it up without heating—
I wonder: would I feel like eating?"

Everyone applauded and laughed, and Professor Bullfinch began, "My dear Joseph, you have a great future before you—"

A voice said, "There they are, Señores."

Into the hotel restaurant came Ramon Almazan followed by five or six men. One of the men, tall and white-haired and with a neat, small beard, stepped forward and bowed.

"Gentlemen," he said, "allow me to present myself. I am Dr. Hernando Guzman, Curator of Archeology of the National Museum of Mexico. These other gentlemen are from the newspapers."

Professor Bullfinch rose and introduced himself and the members of the party.

Dr. Guzman said, "The name of the famous Professor Bullfinch is well known to me, as is also that of Dr. Grimes. When I received your telegram about the Image of the Sun I could not restrain myself from coming at once. Please forgive my bursting in on you, but surely you understand my eagerness to see this wonderful object."

"I do, indeed," said the Professor. "I have it safely stored in the vault of the Bank of No-

mata, and tomorrow morning I will take great pleasure in delivering it to you.''

"I wish we could keep it," Danny put in rather sadly. "It would have been fun to take home a real sunken treasure."

Dr. Guzman regarded him in astonishment. "Fun?" he said. "Take it home? But it is a national treasure—like the Liberty Bell of your own country. We give you our deepest gratitude for finding it."

"Oh, I know that," Danny said hastily. "I was just wishing."

"If it hadn't been for these young people, the Sun Image would still be buried at the bottom of the sea," said the Professor to Dr. Guzman.

"And don't forget Ramon," Joe put in. "Why, without his map we might never have found it."

Ramon grinned. "My uncle said that I must tell you, he only meant the map for a joke. But he is glad you found the treasure. And I have a treasure for you, José. I have saved you half of the drops of root beer."

"My pal," said Joe with a wink.

"It's quite a story," said one of the newspapermen. "Can we get all the details from you, sir?"

The Professor put his hand on Danny's shoulder. "In a moment," he said. "But first, let me tell you, gentlemen—and you, too, Danny, and Joe, and Irene—that we will be taking home a great treasure from the sea, after all."

"What?" cried Joe.

"Another Sun Image?" said Danny.

"Where did you get it?" Irene asked.

"Not another Sun Image," the Professor smiled. "But a treasure just as great and valuable—perhaps more so. You remember my saying that the fish and seaweed in this part of the ocean sometimes grew to great size and were astonishingly healthy? We have suspected some quality of the water, but didn't know what it was.

"And do you remember how the ocean floor was covered with little round things that looked like pebbles? Well, those nodules have been dredged up from many parts of the ocean floor. Scientists have analyzed them and found them to be very rich in important metals like manganese, cobalt, copper, and iron. The nodules are caused by deposits of those metals from the sea water on the shells of tiny animals called *Foraminifera,* after the animals themselves have died.

"When we took the Sun Image aboard, I found that some of the nodules, or pebbles, had come with it. I began an analysis of them and discovered that the nodules in this particular region contain a curious new substance which has been precipitated from the sea water on the shells of the *Foraminifera*. This substance, I believe, has antibiotic qualities—it tends to destroy harmful bacteria, and I believe it may explain the size and health of the creatures and plants in the sea of this region."

He looked benignly around at the amazed

163

faces of his listeners. "You understand what this means?" he went on. "It is a real treasure, one that may help mankind, the treasure of better health and longer life."

"Why, this is wonderful news," said Dr. Guzman. "I congratulate you, my dear Professor."

"Thank you. The credit, however," said the Professor, "must go to our entire group, for we all had a share in the work. And Dr. Grimes, you know, is really the head of this expedition. It was all his idea from the beginning."

Dr. Grimes coughed and bowed.

"Now," the Professor said, taking Dr. Guzman's arm, "if you will come with me to my room, I will show you some photographs we took of the Sun Image this afternoon after coming ashore. Meantime, Dr. Grimes, perhaps you'd be good enough to answer the questions of these newspaper gentlemen."

He led the Mexican archeologist off, and the newsmen crowded round Dr. Grimes. Captain Beaversmith joined them, and he and Dr. Grimes told the story of the descent into the canyon and their adventures on the sea bottom. When they came to the point at which Danny had played the fish recordings, the reporters turned to the boy.

One of them said, "I've never heard any fish sounds before. In fact, I didn't know they made any sounds. Could you play some of these recordings for us?"

"Sure." Danny started for the door. "I'll run up and get my tape recorder."

He was back in a moment or two, and soon had the machine ready. He started it, and they listened in wonder to the soft peeping of the hatchetfish. "Now," said Danny, "I'll play the sound of the viperfish. That's what we used to chase the hatchetfish away, so we could follow them."

He snapped the switch. A high, thin, weird squealing filled the room. The newspapermen clapped their hands over their ears.

Dr. Grimes rubbed his forehead. "Ugh!" he exclaimed. "That noise would scare anything away."

Irene began giggling. "But it's *you*, Dr. Grimes," she said. "Isn't it, Dan? Turn the volume down and listen again."

Danny did as she asked. "She's got the best musical ear of all of us," he said. "And she's right. That's your piccolo."

"But—but it's not possible!" cried Dr. Grimes.

"I'm afraid it is, though," said Danny. "When you used the machine as an amplifier

so you could outplay the Professor, you couldn't
get any sound out of it at first. You must have
been recording then. You recorded your own
playing and that automatically erased the viperfish sounds. So it was you, Dr. Grimes, who
scared away the hatchetfish.''

''And we are all grateful to you, too,'' said
Irene mischievously.

Dr. Grimes frowned. Then his long, severe
face relaxed, and to everyone's surprise, he
grinned widely. ''Well, well,'' he said. ''From
now on, you may call me Pied Piper Grimes.
It certainly is peculiar music.''

"Oh, I don't know," said Joe. "I've heard worse. It's like what our friend Ramon said, once before."

He clapped the Mexican boy on the back.

"Ramon? What did he say?" asked Danny.

"You must develop a taste for it," replied Joe, as everyone laughed. "Like Munchy Chew Bar, no?"

ABOUT THE AUTHORS
AND ILLUSTRATOR

JAY WILLIAMS has written over twenty-five fiction and nonfiction books for children of all ages, in addition to coauthoring fifteen books about Danny Dunn. Mr. Williams was born in Buffalo, New York, and educated at the University of Pennsylvania, Columbia University, and the Art Students League.

RAYMOND ABRASHKIN wrote and coproduced the very popular and successful "Little Fugitive," a film that won an award at the Venice Film Festival.

BRINTON TURKLE was born in Alliance, Ohio. He studied art at the School of the Boston Museum of Fine Arts and the Institute of Design in Chicago. He has been active in the theater, and has both written and illustrated many books for children, including *The Adventures of Obadiah*.